To Hannah
It was fantastic to meet you to

love Megs x

Books by Megs Pritchard

Valentine's Surprise - Standalone Novella

Crossing Desires Series:

Awakening

Struggle

Terrible Twos - Standalone Novel

Take a Chance

Book One

Second Chances series

By

Megs Pritchard

Take a Chance

Book One in the Second Chances series

Copyright © 2017 Megs Pritchard

www.megspritchardauthor.com

Edited by Jessica McKenna - www.liteditor.com

Cover art © Jay Aheer of Simply Defined Art –

www.simplydefinedart.com

All rights reserved. This book is licensed to the original purchaser only.

No part of this publication may be reproduced, distributed, or transmitted in any form or by any means, including photocopying, recording, or other electronic or mechanical methods. It is illegal

and a violation of international copyright law, subject to prosecution and upon conviction, fines and/or imprisonment. Any eBook format cannot legally be loaned or given to others. For permission requests, write to the publisher.

This is a work of fiction. Names, characters, places, and incidents either are the product of the author's imagination or are used fictitiously, and any resemblances to the actual person, living or dead, business establishments, events, or locales is entirely coincidental.

WARNING

This book contains explicit M/M sexual scenes and strong language. It is intended for mature, adult audiences only. Please be aware that this book discusses prostitution with a prostitution act included.

Dedication

To all the people who gave me a glimpse into their lives living on the streets - thank you.

To Helen. Thank you for all the invaluable information you gave me when it came to solicitors. I didn't know how much was involved!

To my amazing and slightly crazy boys. You drive me nuts but I love you. Never change.

Take a Chance

Chapter One

How much longer can I do this for?

Tom Carter sighed as he walked down the street. His shoulders were hunched under his coat, and he moved his hand to grip it tighter around him. He shuddered, goose bumps forming on his skin, and his teeth started to chatter. Sniffing, he bowed his head and watched the rubbish bounce past him. Leaves fluttered in the trees and his ears and eyes stung from the debris in the wind. He blinked them rapidly to try and moisten them. The wind was strong that night.

The overhead lights cast shadows in the dark doorways of the shops, causing Tom to whip his head sharply, looking in as he passed each one. His stomach churned and he sped up, feeling a burn in his chest that radiated out through his limbs. He gulped air in, walking faster.

Tom moved between the puddles that had formed on the pavement.

It had snowed earlier in the day and was now melting. With winter approaching, the weather would worsen, and this meant the possibility of less work for Tom and his friends.

He looked up just in time to avoid a passing car soaking him as it drove through the puddles by the side of the pavement, and Tom stared after it, body tense and hands clenched into fists. Stupid fuck, he thought as he started walking again. The driver didn't give a shit if he had gotten wet or not.

His destination nearing with every step, Tom battled on, knowing that soon he would have his hands wrapped around a mug of hot coffee. He played with the loose change in his pocket, listening to the sounds they made as they fell and hit each other. A cup of coffee was what he considered a luxury when he could afford it, which wasn't often.

Entering the coffee shop and closing the door behind him, Tom took his hands out from his pockets and rubbed them together. He lifted them to his face and blew hot breath on them trying to warm them. He looked around, relaxing his shoulders and rotating them slightly to ease the stiffness. Tom breathed in, smelling the aroma of roasted beans on the air, and the tension fully left him.

He liked the atmosphere and retro style of the coffee shop, from the padded seats to the brown leather sofas and the pictures on the walls of various places around the world. It felt homey and welcoming, like someone was waiting for you with open arms to hold you close. He felt the warmth enter him and closed his eyes before opening them and looking towards the counter.

Tom strolled up to place his order, smiling when he recognised who was stood behind the counter. "Hi, Sam, the usual please."

"Hey, Tom, not looking too good out there now, is it?" Sam asked him, smiling.

Take a Chance

"Nope, and it looks like more sleet too," Tom answered as he quickly looked back out of the shop windows.

"Aw, shit, man, just what I needed," Sam muttered as he picked up the coffee filter handle.

"Bad day?"

"You know, just because I work in a coffee shop doesn't mean I'm stupid, but for some reason, certain people come in here and speak to me like I'm a piece of shit. No manners and half the time they don't stop talking on their phone or doing whatever they're doing like Facebook or Twitter or some other shit. Sometimes they don't even look up at you, just order in the 'I'm better than you' voice. It pisses me off, but I smile and keep my mouth shut and take their order." Sam shook his head.

Tom smiled. "Not for much longer though. Isn't this your final year?"

"Yeah, but I'm thinking of doing my Masters, so who knows."

"Fuck, more punishment? Haven't you had enough?" Tom asked him as he raised his eyebrows.

Sam smiled. "Obviously not." Sam continued to make Tom's coffee. "We're quiet tonight, so why don't you sit down and I'll bring it over to you."

Tom nodded. "Okay, here's the money."

"Thanks."

Tom skirted around the tables and chairs until he sat at an empty table by the window. He watched some teenagers go by, laughing and splashing each other with water kicked up from the puddles. Tom smiled wistfully to himself as his shoulders dropped and he stared down at his hands. Had he ever been that carefree? Could he even remember the feeling? Not now. His shoulders tensed and his hands clenched together on the table as he took a deep shuddering breath in.

"Here you go," Sam commented as he placed the cup of coffee on the table in front of him.

"Thanks, mate." Tom smiled at him.

"No worries," Sam replied as walked back to the counter, stopping to pick up an empty cup on his way.

Tom turned to the window again and caught his reflection in it. Shaggy long blond hair and blue eyes with a strong jaw stared back at him. He looked tired with dark circles under his eyes and hollow cheeks. God, he was so tired that he wasn't sure if he could continue anymore. He closed his eyes briefly, rubbing his forehead as he contemplated what he was going to do. His body sagged and he opened his eyes to stare out of the window again. With this weather and the drop in temperature, he doubted there'd be much work for him tonight, but you never know, someone might be looking for some action. For some reason, certain individuals came out looking for a fuck regardless of the weather. Or, he could just head back to the abandoned house he and his friends were currently living in and relax instead. But, he would need some money if the weather was going to stay the way it was. Another option would be to pick someone's pockets, but he hated doing that. He wasn't a thief and stealing handbags or wallets wasn't something he wanted to resort to doing. But it didn't change the fact that if the weather continued, then he might have to do just that.

He stared down into his coffee as he thought about what he was going to do. He didn't know how long he could keep doing this, how long he could carry on living like this. This life was all he had known since he was fifteen and his parents had kicked him out for being gay. He'd only had the clothes he'd been wearing and some loose change in his pocket. Now he was living hand to mouth, and with no education, that wasn't likely to change.

Take a Chance

Sighing, Tom picked up his cup, draining the coffee. Putting it back down on the table, he stood and waved to Sam. As he was turning to leave, a group of people came into the shop, bumping into him. Tom apologised, but apart from a hard stare, they ignored him and continued walking to the counter. Ignorant bastards, he thought as he walked over to the door.

Tom left the coffee shop and started to walk down the street, looking over his shoulder to make sure no one had followed him out. His heart was pounding in his chest, and his palms were sweaty. He turned a corner and took his hand out of his pocket, holding a wallet. Smiling to himself, he opened it and looked through the contents. It held the usual items: driver's license, cash and credit cards. A hundred quid and some loose change. Enough to see him through the next few days if he was careful. He let out a huge breath as he rubbed the notes between his fingers, feeling the texture of the paper. He brought them to his nose and inhaled their fragrance and closed his eyes as he muttered, "Thanks."

Looking for a bin, he threw the wallet in and continued walking along the street, making his way to his current home. He hunched up again under his thin coat as he felt the chill in the air work its way through him. Again, he thought about the life he was leading, his 'job'. He humourlessly laughed to himself. Who was he kidding? He was a rent boy, a hooker, getting paid for hand jobs, blow jobs and fucks. At least he always used condoms. He needed to stay clean and couldn't pass anything on. He had some guys who came to him on a regular basis, family men, men making lots of money, going places. Why they would want to fuck a rent boy was beyond him, but who was he to question it? They paid; that was all that mattered. Four long years of doing this and there seemed to be no end in sight. There was no knight in shining armour to rescue him and take him away from this life. He just had to get through the day, and then the next, then the next. That's how he had to look at it.

Spotting the abandoned house further along the road, Tom turned off and walked through the alley to the rear of the property. He gagged slightly at the noxious odour of decaying food that littered the ground. He looked for the loose panel on the fence at the back, eager to escape the rancid smell. Pulling it back slightly, he crawled through and sped up the path to the back door, where another loose panel was, and squeezed his way through that one.

Once inside, he felt his body relax, and his stomach finally settle. He walked through the kitchen, cupboards hanging from the walls, black grout between the once white tiles, and stepped carefully over the curling lino on the floor. A stale odour hung in the air as he continued to the lounge. When he walked in, he found Luke and Matt sitting on the floor sharing a bag of chips.

Both looked up at him as he entered, and Luke smiled. "What's up?"

There were five of them that lived together in the house, all doing the same thing. Matt and Luke were younger than him, and when he had run into them one night, he couldn't leave them sitting in a doorway freezing. He'd sat and had spoken with them for a while, getting to know them, and eventually they'd started hanging around together, looking out for each other. Now they lived together.

Matt and Luke had contrasting looks. Matt had spiky brown hair with hazel eyes while Luke was blond, hair kept short and blue eyed.

"Not much. Too shitty to go out tonight, so I'm givin' it a miss. What're you two doing? Going out later?"

Both shook their heads. "Nah, same as you. Not a good night to go out. Adam and Ben are out, but that was more Adam. Ben just tagged along to make sure he was safe, you know," Matt replied, looking up at him.

"I'm surprised they've gone out. It won't be long 'til it's pissing down."

"Adam needs the money, with him being ill earlier in the week. He was adamant he was going, and we couldn't get him to change his mind. He's determined to make some cash," Luke advised. "All he had to do was ask. One of us would have chipped in to help him out. It's not like we hadn't done it before when one of us has been sick."

Tom snorted. "You know what Adam's like - he doesn't like relying on anyone. At least he took Ben with him, so he's not alone." Tom paused. "When did they go out?" Tom pinched his lips together as he scrubbed his hand over his face.

Matt turned to Luke and frowned. "Couple of hours ago now, wouldn't you say?"

Luke nodded while he ate some chips. "Yeah, didn't say how long they would be gone for, but I can't imagine it would be for too long though. You can hear the wind." He swallowed and looked at Tom. "Want some chips?"

"Nah, it's okay. I had a coffee on the way back. I was lucky, as I was leaving I bumped into some blokes, and now I'm a bit richer. Hoping it will keep us all goin' for a couple of days until the weather improves. Honestly, don't want to be out in this weather." He rubbed the back of his neck as he rolled his shoulders. The cold in the room was beginning to sink into his flesh.

Tom headed towards the door, looking over his shoulder at Matt and Luke. "I'm heading up. I'll see you guys later." He walked out as he heard the other two say "night" to him. He walked along the hallway towards the stairs and slowly stepped up them, trailing his fingers along the banister as he did. He felt bits of paint fall off and heard his footsteps echo throughout. Looking around the house, he was met with peeling wallpaper, cracked and chipped paint, and damp patches on the ceiling and running down the walls. The air was chilly and had a musty odour to it, which he tried not to breathe in too deeply. When he was in the room he and the others were sharing, he looked around and exhaled, not realising he'd been holding his breath. Yeah, this life was getting old, but with nothing else on the horizon, this was all he had. He sat down slowly on his old, ratty sleeping bag and took out the money he had stolen earlier, counting through it again. There was enough for them all to keep going for a couple for days.

Sighing, Tom slowly lay down and stared up at the ceiling, noticing the familiar cracks and peeling paint and water stains. He could smell the damp in the air and the chill as it permeated the building and into him. Rolling over onto his side, he looked at his meagre belongings and curled up as tightly as he could, squeezing his eyes shut. *Fuck it. I can't keep doing this, but what other options do I have?*

As he lay there, he heard the sounds of the others talking from below followed by shouting. "Tom! Tom, get down here now, something's happened to Adam."

❋ ❋ ❋

Tom leapt up from his makeshift bed, heart pounding in his chest, and ran out of his room, jumping down the stairs until he reached the bottom.

Entering the lounge, Tom could see Ben stood in the middle of the room, running his hands through his dark-brown hair repeatedly as he paced the floor. "He was only out of my sight for a fuckin' minute, if that," he was saying. "Fuck," Ben shouted as he grabbed his hair, pulling at it.

Tom's mouth filled with saliva and he turned, finding Adam lying on the floor covered in blood, curled up on his side in a foetal position. Arms wrapped around his stomach, Adam moaned softly as he shivered. His clothes were soaked and ripped in several places. The water from his wet hair ran into the blood on his face, making it look worse. Tom rushed over to him, dropping to his knees beside him and gently lifting his head up to look at his face. Adam groaned and tried to pull away.

"No, Adam, I need to see ya face. You might need to go the hospital." Tom's hands shook as he quickly scanned Adam's face, and his stomach churned at the damage he could see.

Adam shook his head, wincing as he did. "No hospital. Just patch me up."

"For fuck's sake, Adam, that cut above your eye needs stitches, not to mention the other injuries," Ben shouted. "Look, we can say you got jumped walking home. No one needs to know what went down."

"And where would I tell 'em I live, Ben? What do you think –?"

"He's fuckin' right, Adam," Tom interrupted. "You need to go. Ben and I'll take you. Don't argue about it," Tom ordered as Adam started to protest. "We'll hail a taxi and go."

"And how can we afford a cab, huh? I've hardly made any fuckin' money tonight."

"It doesn't matter. We can't walk to the hospital. It's just too far." Tom looked over at Matt and Luke. "You guys stay here. Come on, Ben, help me get him up."

Ben came over and got hold of Adam's right arm with Tom grabbing his left. Tom could see blood in Adam's auburn hair, and his throat tightened when he thought about how much pain Adam must be feeling. Together, they managed to get Adam onto his feet. Ben held onto him while Tom put Adam's arm over his shoulder, and then copied the action. Tom turned to the others. "We'll be back as soon as we can." Tom rubbed Adam's back in an attempt to soothe him.

Both nodded and Matt walked over to them. Staring at Adam, he told him, "You're doing the right thing." Glancing at Ben and Tom, he said, "Take care of him and don't take any of his bullshit."

"Hey," Adam said.

Ignoring him, Tom nodded. "Let's go, Ben."

Together, they slowly walked Adam out of the lounge into the hallway and then the kitchen. Luke appeared and held the board up to allow them to get through. "Take care, mate," he whispered to Adam as he hugged him. They eased Adam through the gap and then heard the board being put back in place. They walked and dragged Adam down the path towards the broken fence panel, again easing him through until all three had made it out. They slowly made their way along the alley and onto the street looking for a taxi to hail. Tom was starting to breathe heavily and could feel sweat gathering on his brow.

"D'ya think we'll be lucky enough to have one just sat there waiting?" Ben asked.

Tom grunted. "I'll think we'll have better luck the closer to the city centre we get. Is there a phone box around here?"

Ben shook his head. "Not that common now, what with all the smartphones around, but you never know, we might get lucky, or someone will stop and offer us a lift."

"Really, ya think?" scoffed Tom.

"Hey, I still believe there are good people out there, ya know."

"I wish I did." Tom grunted.

Ben smiled. "I believe in the good in people."

Adam groaned. "Will you two shut the fuck up and just get me to the fuckin' hospital. I don't give a shit 'bout the good in people."

Take a Chance

"Okay, mate, we'll get there as soon as we can," Tom muttered.

They continued to walk along the street, searching for a passing taxi that they could flag down. Tom bit his lip and tightened his grip on Adam's arm as he staggered under Adam's weight. Fortunately, luck was on their side and a black cab drove by. Tom waved frantically to draw the driver's attention and blew out a breath when it slowed to a stop next to them.

Once they got Adam settled, Tom leaned forward. "Nearest hospital."

The driver looked back at them and took in Adam's appearance. He frowned before asking, "What happened to him?"

"He was jumped on his way home," Ben murmured.

"Can you just get us there as quick as possible, please?" Tom asked.

"Sure, it'll only take a couple of minutes."

The taxi drove quickly through the streets, and five minutes later, pulled up outside Accident and Emergency. The driver turned to them and reached his hand out. "That'll be a fiver."

Tom pulled out a tenner and handed it over, bouncing his leg as he waited for his change while Ben got Adam out of the taxi. Once he had his change, Tom got out and stood outside A & E with Ben and Adam.

Looking across the car park to the entrance, Tom took a deep breath in and straightened.

"Come on, let's get in there. Fuck, I hope it isn't busy."

Chapter Two

They entered A & E, and the noise hit them. People were talking simultaneously, some shouting. Names were being called out, and someone was crying. The smell of disinfectant and smoke and vomit stung Tom's nostrils, and he tried to breathe through his mouth instead. He squinted his eyes against the bright overhead lighting as his eyes watered. It was painfully bright after being outside in the dark.

Queuing for the reception so they could register Adam, Ben turned to Tom and asked, "How we doin' this? What are we gonna say?"

Tom searched Ben's face, noticing his wrinkled brow. He looked around to make sure no one could hear them. "I'm not sure. We could say we found him like this and brought him in or say we don't know where he lives. I don't know." He rubbed his hand down his pants to remove the sweat that had suddenly appeared on them. He scanned the crowd repeatedly, making sure there were no police around.

Take a Chance

"Hey, I know. You could just let me answer the fuckin' questions. I'm the one who's fuckin' injured," Adam interrupted. "I can say 'no fixed abode'. I'm sure they've heard it before."

Tom looked at Adam and flushed. "Sorry, mate."

Adam snorted but didn't reply as he stared ahead, clenching his jaw.

They continued to wait in the queue until they reached the desk. Tom left Adam to deal with the registering process while he scanned the waiting area. There were a variety of people already waiting and by the number of them, it looked like they would be waiting some time. He looked up at the monitor and could see that the estimated waiting time was three hours. Tom groaned and rubbed a hand over his face as he looked up at the ceiling while shaking his head. He nudged Ben and nodded his head towards the time. "Seen how long the wait is?" he asked.

Ben turned and looked at it, also groaning. "Great, just how I want to spend my fuckin' Sunday night."

Adam looked over his shoulder at them and grunted. "Hey, at least you're pain-free though. Come on and help me over to some chairs."

Four hours later, Adam was eventually called in to see a nurse, which was followed by some x-rays, precautionary, and then the long wait for the doctor. After five and a half hours, some stitches for the cut above his eye and two fractured fingers strapped up, Adam was released with painkillers and advice to rest for a few days. They managed to hail a cab and within twenty minutes were back on their street, making the slow walk back to the house.

They walked in to find Matt and Luke asleep in the lounge. Both woke up to the sound of them entering the room and immediately started asking questions.

"What did the hospital say?"

"How are you?"

Adam held up his hands and smiled. "Hey, I'm okay really. Some stitches, painkillers and rest and I'll be back to normal. I'm more worried about money and when I can get back out. Need some cash."

"We can sort that in the morning. Get some rest. It's been a long night. Nothing tires you out more than sitting on your arse doing nothing," Tom said.

Tom left the lounge and walked upstairs. In the bathroom, he stopped and stared at himself in the mirror, then dropped his head. His body felt heavy, and it was difficult to raise his head again. He cleaned up, then crawled into his sleeping bag. He lay there thinking about how lucky Adam had been. If Ben had taken a couple of seconds longer, then Adam could have been driven off somewhere, and fuck knows what would have happened to him. Things were starting to get rough out there, and they were going to have to be extra vigilant when they were working. His stomach tightened at the thought of what was happening out on the streets, and his heart started to beat harder and faster. He closed his eyes and breathed deeply, trying to slow his body down. He shook out his arms and legs and then stretched before rolling onto his side and curling up.

He stared at the wall and reached out to touch the crumbling plaster. It felt moist and tacky when he rubbed it between his fingers, almost clay-like in substance. He wiped his fingers on the floor but realised all he had done was transfer the grime onto them. He rolled onto his back and squeezed his eyes tightly shut. One day, he would open them, and he wouldn't be in this room, he would be somewhere better. His eyes itched and burned, and he blinked rapidly, refusing to let the tears fall.

※ ※ ※

Take a Chance

The next morning, Tom woke to find all the others except Adam sleeping. He stood, stretched and then listened. Hearing nothing but the breathing of the others in the room, he rubbed his arms to try and keep what little warmth he had in them as he tip-toed out. After taking a leak in the bathroom, he went downstairs, carefully avoiding the steps that creaked. He found Adam sitting in the lounge, leaning back against the wall, staring blankly at the wall opposite him. He watched him and felt a chill run through his body as he thought about the previous night's events. Again, his stomach churned at the thought of what could have happened to Adam had Ben not been there.

"Didn't expect you to be up so soon," he commented as he walked into the room. The hairs on his arms stood up as the chill in the room hit his exposed skin. He should have worn a jumper.

"Pain woke me, so I came down."

"Have you taken some of ya meds?"

"Yeah, just waitin' for 'em to kick in."

Tom took a deep breath, then asked, "What happened last night?"

Adam shrugged. "I was fuckin' stupid. Should've waited for Ben but didn't wanna lose the guy. I should've checked out the car before goin' over 'cause I didn't see the fuckin' passenger."

"So you decided to go for it, even though Ben wasn't there and wouldn't be able to remember the car details. Really, Adam? It's not like you to do something like that." Tom paused before asking, "What else happened?"

"Really? You wanna know all the fuckin' details?" Adam snapped, glaring at Tom, his blue eyes cold and flat.

"Course I do. Someone tried to kidnap you! If Ben hadn't been there, do you think we'd be fucking' talking now? For fuck's sake, Adam, you could've been beaten unconscious, raped or even fuckin' murdered! You know these attacks are getting worse. We need to stick together and keep an eye on each other and check the cars out before we get in!" Tom fisted his hands as he glared at Adam.

"Hey, okay, look, I know I was fuckin' stupid. If you must know, Ben had gone for a leak, and he was only gonna be a couple of minutes, if that, so I wasn't worried, you know. This car pulls up. I took a look at it and decided to go over. The guy wound his window down and waved to me. As soon I leaned in, he grabbed me and tried to drag me in the car. I started to shout and hit out at anythin' I could. The passenger had gotten hold of me, and the fuckin' driver was trying to get away." Adam glanced away as he swallowed. "I grabbed the handbrake and put it on, so the driver was fuckin' punchin' me with one hand and trying to get the handbrake off with the other. The passenger had hold of me hair and was yanking me head back to try and punch me. Ben came charging out, shouting, and he grabs me legs and pulls me out of the window. The car takes off at that point."

Tom's mouth fell open as he stared incredulously at Adam. "Shit, there's two of them working together?" he gasped out. Fuck. One person was bad enough, but two?

Adam shook his head. "We don't know that it's the same fuckers attacking us, do we? It could've been a couple of twats wantin' to do some gay bashing."

"A bit of a coincidence though, isn't it? Did you get any details of the car? Make, model, reg?"

"Black, newish model, possibly a Toyota or a Honda." Adam shrugged. "They look similar, but I couldn't tell ya which one for certain. As for the reg? Nothing, I didn't see it all. Maybe Ben did, but I was lookin' floor at that point, so nothing." Adam shook his head.

"At least we have something, right? We let the others know what to look out for, and if they cross paths with anyone else, they can pass that info on. I don't need to tell you that we need to look out for each other because no fucker else is doing it for us," Tom explained.

They were both silent for a few minutes, then Tom asked, "You know what worries me?"

Adam shook his head. "What?"

"These attacks are gettin' worse, you know. A guy getting punched in the face is one thing, but to try and force someone into a car..." Tom trailed off. What next? When would it stop? "At least you'll be staying in for a few days to recover. No, don't say anything," Tom asked, as Adam went to interrupt him. "You heard what the doc said about taking a few days, and let's be honest you're not gonna get much work looking like that. Well, I'd hope not, but you never know what kinks some blokes have."

"Hey, I've got to work. I'm almost broke. Sure, I had a good run over the weekend, but that's not gonna fuckin' last, is it? I can't have you guys tryin' to help me out."

"I've got enough to last a few days if we're careful. We'll sort something out. I'm not sure if we should be goin' out for a few days. They didn't get you last night, so fuck knows if and when they'll try again. We should stay away for a few days, then think about it again, maybe towards the weekend."

Adam slowly stood. "You're overreacting. I know I have to rest, but after that? I'm out, alright?"

Tom stood as well, shaking his head as he reached a hand out towards Adam. "I'm not over--"

Adam shoved Tom. "Shut the fuck up, Tom. I get it, 'cause you're older than us, you think you're some kind of fuckin' leader, seem to think you're in fuckin' charge, but you're not. So quit telling me what the fuck to do, right? I get to decide when I'm fit to go out, not you." Adam turned away from Tom and started walking out of the lounge. "I don't wanna talk about this shit again and don't even think of tellin' this to the others 'cause I'll be fuckin' pissed. You don't want to be around me when I'm like that. Got it?"

Tom took a step back, eyes widening. Yes, he thought he was responsible. He'd been on the streets the longest and had managed to keep relatively safe. He hadn't fallen to the temptation of drugs, though there had been more than enough opportunities, and let's be honest, plenty of times when he wanted to forget the shithole that was his life. He'd seen and heard enough, more than the others, and he just wanted to keep them all safe. He grabbed his hair and looked up at the ceiling as he breathed deeply. Grabbing his jacket, he made his way out of the house to get some fresh air and clear his head.

By Wednesday, Adam had decided that he'd waited long enough to recover and was going back out, even with everyone asking him to wait a little bit longer.

Tom sat on the floor watching, feeling the coldness seep through the back of his jeans, and listened to the others trying to convince Adam to rest for another day. His stomach churned with the knowledge that he couldn't keep Adam safe. He wouldn't be surprised if Adam left them soon, doing his own thing. But if Adam left, then Ben would too.

Tom picked up a small stone of the floor and let it fall from between his fingers. Things had been tense between them since their fallout on Monday, so he knew nothing he said would change Adam's mind.

"I'll go with you if you're certain this is what you wanna do," Ben was saying. "I agree with the others though. Wait another day."

Take a Chance

Adam shook his head while checking his supplies. "Nope, not gonna happen. I've wasted fuckin' days already, sittin' in here doing fuck all. I need to get back out there and hit the streets. This is fuckin' Manchester. There's always action somewhere, and Wednesday's as good a night as any other. You guys know that. I need the money. I can't keep relying on you." Adam put his jacket on, checking his pockets again. He turned to Ben, asking, "Ya ready then?"

Ben stared at his feet and sighed before he finally nodded. "Yeah, but we're not stayin' out too long. You've still not fully recovered."

"Whatever," Adam muttered over his shoulder as he left the room.

Tom stood up and walked over to Ben. "Keep an eye on him tonight. He doesn't give a shit that he was almost kidnapped a couple of days ago. I don't like the way he's acting at the moment." He looked out the door that Adam had just walked through and frowned as he pursed his lips.

"You and me both." Ben lifted his hand to Matt and Luke as he left the room.

"I don't think there was anything else we could've said to make him stay, Tom. He wants to get back out there," Matt muttered, shaking his head.

"What about you two?" Tom asked.

Luke looked up at him. "We're listening to you on this. If you say we should wait 'til Friday, then we wait. You've been doing this longer than we have and to be honest? We're grateful you took us in when you did." Luke shook his head. "I don't know how much longer we would have managed without you being there to help us."

Tom jerked his head back as his eyes opened wide when he heard Luke. "Er, okay, thanks." He ducked his head and stared at the floor as his cheeks flushed. He never expected anyone to say something like that to him.

"Yeah, well, we mean it, and on that note, we're gonna get something to eat. Want anything?" Matt asked as he and Luke stood up, getting ready to go out.

Tom shook his head. "Nah, I'm good, thanks."

"Alright, see ya in a few."

Tom sat on the floor as he watched them leave and heard them go out back, wondering again how those two had ended up on the streets. He knew they had finished school, but after that, nothing. He let his head drop back and hit the wall as he stared up at the paint peeling from the ceiling. He could feel the coldness of the room on his skin, causing goose bumps to appear, and he shivered in an attempt to keep warm. Events were occurring on the streets, and he didn't know what to do about it or how to keep everyone safe, and he did feel like they were his responsibility, especially Matt and Luke. His shoulders sagged, hands falling limply to his sides as he tried to swallow past the lump that had developed in his throat.

Chapter Three

Sebastian Banks sat at his desk at work and looked at the clock...again. The day was dragging and there seemed to be no end in sight. He sighed and started to read the document again as he rubbed his fingers over his chin, but still he couldn't make it past the third paragraph without wondering what he'd just read. Clearly, he wasn't taking any of it in.

Sitting back in his chair, Seb dropped the document on the desk and stood, reaching for his empty mug. Maybe some coffee would help. He walked along the corridor and entered the break area. Grabbing the carafe of coffee, he filled his mug and sat on the black leather sofa, sinking in deeply as he let the heat from the mug absorb into his hands. He wrapped them around it and slowly brought it to his face. He inhaled the aroma of freshly brewed coffee and took a tentative sip, tasting the bitterness on his tongue and feeling the heat flood his mouth.

Seb looked around the room. It was bright and airy with cream walls and a couple of tables and chairs. It contained a small kitchen area, with a microwave and coffee machine. Seb smiled. This place ran on coffee, and he knew he couldn't function without at least a couple himself. He needed that java wake up call.

Hearing footsteps approaching, he looked towards the doorway to see who was coming. "Oh, hi Geoff, how's your day going?" Geoff was the co-owner of the company.

Tall with thick black hair and startling grey eyes, Geoff was a genuinely nice guy.

"Better than yours by the looks of it. Late night?" Geoff smiled, his grey eyes sparkling.

"A little." He chuckled. "I popped 'round some friends last night to have a catch up and ended staying later than I'd planned."

Geoff laughed. "And now you're paying for it."

Seb watched Geoff walk over to the coffee pot and pour one for himself. He turned to Seb, leaning back on the counter.

"Yep. I need caffeine and lots of it."

"I was going to come over and see you at some point today. Your two-year contract is going to end soon, and I wanted to talk to you about your future here."

Seb inhaled sharply as his hands tightened around the mug. "Should I be worried?"

"It's all good Seb. You've done great work here, and we're happy to have you. So when you're free, come over and see me, and don't worry, alright?"

"Yeah, okay," Seb replied, frowning slightly.

Geoff smiled and walked from the room, leaving Seb sat there. He chewed his bottom lip as he ran his hand through his hair. His mouth was suddenly dry, and he took a sip of his coffee to moisten it. He had gone through four years of Uni, a year on a Legal Practice Course and then been fortunate to be employed at Fosters Solicitors, a small but prestigious company, for his two-year training contract. Now that was ending, he had decisions to make.

Seb liked it at Fosters. The people he worked with were friendly and had been wonderful when he'd first started, showing him the ropes and helping him to fit in. He'd become more comfortable and confident in his abilities. That wasn't to say he hadn't made mistakes, fortunately, nothing serious, but overall he felt that he had performed well enough to earn a full-time position.

Seb stood and ambled back to his desk, his mind on the meeting with Geoff. Geoff had been the first person he had met when he walked through the door on his first day and had instantly liked him. He was friendly, approachable and was always ready to help out. Geoff would listen to Seb while he discussed the cases he worked on and offer advice if he needed it. He always had a smile on his face, and Seb found him attractive with his grey eyes and black hair.

Sitting at his desk, he picked up the discarded document but found it even harder to read. He stared absently out of the window, watching the clouds move slowly across the sky. What did Geoff want to speak to him about?

Looking back at the document, Seb again attempted to read it but after reading the same paragraph several times and still not remembering any of it, he decided to find out what Geoff had to say.

Seb stood, his stomach churning, and walked over to Geoff's office, noticing that Geoff's personal assistant, Lisa, wasn't at her desk. Knocking on the open door when he got there, Seb rubbed his sweaty palms on his pants waiting for Geoff to answer.

"Come in," Geoff instructed, smiling when he saw it was Seb. "Didn't think it would be too long before you showed up."

Seb smiled and shrugged. "Is it a good time for that talk?" he asked.

"Sure. Come in and take a seat. Let me just close this document down. Oh, can you shut the door as well."

Seb walked into the room, closing the door behind him, and took a seat in the chair across from Geoff's. He looked around the room, noticing the bookcase that took up one wall, filled with books regarding laws, policies and procedures. The room was clearly masculine with dark-brown furniture and cream walls and a pale cream carpet. Pictures of friends and family decorated the room, and Seb could see the resemblance between Geoff and his father. The room had a warm calmness to it that settled his churning stomach.

"Alright, all done. Thanks for waiting." Geoff leaned forward on his desk, watching Seb. "So, we would like you to stay with us. The work you've done the last two years has been excellent, and you've picked up the way we work here and have fitted in easily. If you want the job, it's yours. I can have Rita in HR sort out the contract details." Geoff looked at Seb's shocked face and smiled. "Did you think I was going to say something else?"

"I'm just surprised, I guess. I mean, yes, thanks, I would love to stay here. Thank you." Seb grinned widely.

"Great. I'll call Rita and let her know, and we'll get the contract sorted." Geoff stood and held his hand out.

Seb also stood and shook his hand, still a little surprised he now had a full-time permanent job. "I'll just get back to it then," he mumbled.

"Alright. I'll no doubt see you later. Leave the door open on your way out, will you?"

Take a Chance

"Yes, and thanks again."

Seb left the room and walked back to his desk with a spring in his step and a smile on his face. Suddenly, his day was a whole lot better, and that document? It was easy to read now.

When it was time to leave, Seb closed down his computer and tidied his desk. Grabbing his jacket and bag, he strolled out of the office, waving at the few people still working. As he walked past reception, he waved to Mel, the receptionist. "Bye, see ya tomorrow, Mel."

"Hey. What're your plans for tonight, hun?" Mel asked him.

"Not much," Seb said with a shrug. "Gym then home. What about you?"

"That depends on you, hun. Fancy grabbing a meal?"

Seb stopped and looked at Mel. Five-foot-nothing, blonde hair and big brown eyes, she was very attractive, just not his type. She was also a notorious man-eater. He smiled at her while he shook his head. "Weren't you seeing someone? What happened there? I thought it was all hot and heavy?"

Mel sighed while she waved a hand in front of her face. "He wants more, like what we have isn't enough. I told him on our first date I didn't do serious, but you know, he just couldn't help himself. What I need is a fuck buddy. Know any?" Mel looked up at him, batting her eyelashes suggestively.

Seb's body tensed and a cold sweat broke out over his skin at the thought that Mel wanted him for a possible fuck buddy. He liked her, yeah, but soooo not like that. He stammered out, "Er, no, sorry. Anyway, got to go. I'll see you in the morning." He shouted the last part over his shoulder as he practically jogged to the lifts hoping one was on their floor.

When one opened, Seb rushed in and hit the button repeatedly. Glancing out, he saw Mel sat at reception frowning as she watched him. He waved and smiled as the doors closed. Sighing in relief, Seb leaned back, closing his eyes. Finally the work day was over.

※ ※ ※

Exiting the building, Seb walked towards the local gym. The air was crisp with an underlying smell of car fumes and cigarette smoke. When he reached the gym, he changed into his workout gear, threw his bag into a locker, put his headphones in, and started his workout. Running for thirty minutes, followed by twenty on the rowing machine, and then the free weights. Over an hour after he had started, he finished and headed for his locker. Walking back into the locker room, Seb noticed that it had been refurbished recently, which he had somehow missed when he'd first come in. Light blue and white tiles on the walls and new black tiled effect flooring. It was quiet in the room, and Seb sat on the bench with an audible grunt as he rolled his shoulders back, wincing at the ache.

Stripping quickly, Seb walked towards the showers. After his shower, he noticed a hot blond guy looking him up and down smiling. Seb smiled back, and the blond came over. A few whispered words were all that was needed, and Seb was back in the shower with the blond guy on his knees sucking his dick like a Hoover. Man, he was good.

Grabbing blond guy's hair, he used it to hold his head still while he fucked his mouth. The blond guy knew what he was doing. Grabbing the base of his cock, he swirled his tongue around his head while rolling his balls with his other hand. Next, he bobbed his head up and down, never losing the suction he had on his cock. Seb felt that familiar tingling that said his orgasm was coming, and then jerked as he emptied himself into the blond guy's mouth. He leaned back against the wall while catching his breath. Blond started kissing his way up his stomach and chest, and as he went to kiss his mouth, Seb pulled back with a smile and dropped to his knees. He was a firm believer that both people should get off.

Just then, the door opened to the changing rooms, and Seb could hear laughter from a group of guys who had come in. He stood up and smiled. "Maybe another time," he muttered as he left the shower stall.

Seb walked to his locker and got dressed. Looking in the mirror, he stared at his reflection for a minute. Black hair and deep brown eyes stared back at him. Not too bad looking. Shrugging, he threw his gym gear and toiletries into his bag and left, walking over to the car park where his car was.

Seb loved his car. It was the second most expensive thing he'd bought apart from his house after leaving Uni. His baby was a black Golf. Nothing too fancy, but she was all his and he took care of her. Getting in, he started the engine and headed home.

Traffic wasn't too heavy, so it was only twenty minutes later before he pulled onto the driveway of his house and he sighed deeply. Looking at his house, he smiled. He'd been able to use his inheritance money and some money his parents had given him to buy it. It needed a lot of work doing to it, which was why he'd been able to get it so cheap. He would never have been able to afford a house in this area if the house had been in good condition. But, he was willing to put in the time and effort needed to get the house back to a family home.

Picking up his gym bag, Seb got out of his car and locked it as he walked to the door. Entering, he picked up his mail and quickly scanned it. It was either bills or junk. He threw it on the counter in the kitchen and then opened his freezer to see what he had to eat. Grabbing a ready meal, he popped it in the microwave and switched it on. As the food was cooking, he popped the kettle on and then emptied his gym bag.

Once his food was cooked and plated, Seb walked into the lounge and sat down on the sofa. He turned the TV on and watched it while he ate. Halfway through his meal, his phone rang. Reaching over, he picked it up. "Hello," he answered.

"Hello, son. I thought I'd call seen as I haven't heard from you all week," his mother, Kath, commented.

Seb internally groaned as he tensed at hearing his mother's voice. As much as he loved his parents, they interfered far too much in his life. It was almost like they couldn't accept the fact that he was an adult now with a life of his own.

"Hi Mum. How are you and dad?"

"We're both fine, son. Just wanted to make sure you're alright and still coming over on Sunday for lunch? Will you be bringing someone with you?"

And that was the real reason for the call. He closed his eyes as he frowned. They were always asking about girls he knew or if there was a special woman in his life and when he was going to bring one home. He was twenty-four, almost twenty-five, so he wasn't ready to settle down yet, and he didn't think it would be with a woman. Not that there was anything wrong with women; he was bisexual, so he had been with both men and women. The problem was he hadn't told his parents he was bisexual. They went to church every Sunday and were a large part of that community and were always making comments about gays and their lifestyle like it was a choice to be gay. He knew they loved him, but he wasn't sure if it would be enough when he told them his sexual preferences. So, for now, he just kept quiet.

"I'll be over on Sunday, Mum. Usual time?"

"Of course dear. Will we need to set the table for four?" Seb moved the phone away as he muttered 'for fucks sake' quietly.

When he placed the phone back to his ear, he asked, "Is Josh not coming?"

"No, he's busy with Uni, dear, you know that. Hopefully next weekend. So four places?"

"No, Mum, it'll just be me." Seb waited. He was certain his mum would have something to say, and he was right.

"Now Sebastian, you need to find a nice young lady. You're not getting any younger. You know, your father and I were already married at your age and--"

Seb dropped his head into his free hand and shook his head. "I know, Mum, but I'm busy with work, which reminds me. I've been offered a full-time job." Seb interrupted her, hoping to change the conversation.

"Really! That's wonderful news. I'll have to let the women know when I see them tomorrow for the church meeting."

"I'm going to get going, Mum, because I'm just having my tea right now, so I'll see you Sunday."

"Alright son, and just let me know if I need to add another place for lunch."

"Alright, I will do. Bye."

"Goodbye, son."

Seb dropped the phone on the sofa beside him and leaned his head back, closing his eyes. Sometimes the phone calls with his mum could be draining, even if they were relatively short. He looked down at his meal and frowned as he pushed the food around his plate and decided he wasn't hungry. Switching the TV off, he walked into the kitchen and threw his food in the bin. He went upstairs to the bathroom, where he washed, brushed his teeth and took a leak. Getting into bed, it wasn't long before he was asleep.

❋ ❋ ❋

Friday was pretty much the same as Thursday for Seb except for the moment when he received his new contract from Rita. His cheeks ached due to the constant smile he had on his face, and he had an extra bounce in his walk. He was looking forward to going out with his friends tonight and celebrating.

As soon as work had finished, Seb drove home to shower and change. Work had run over, Seb dealing with a new case, so he was running late. As he was staying over at a friend's apartment, which was roughly thirty minutes away and near the city centre, he knew he would be almost an hour before he got there. Seb sent a quick text to let Gary know he was going to be late and got in his car.

As Seb was driving through the streets towards Gary's, he saw a group of what looked like teenagers standing on the street, and it was obvious what they were doing. As he drove past, he couldn't help but look at them and noticed how young some of them seemed. Shaking his head sadly, he drove on but suddenly realised one of them looked familiar. He carried on driving but had a strange hollow sensation in the pit of his stomach, and for some reason, he decided to turn around and drive back towards the group.

Seb slowed down as he neared them, and one of the individuals separated from the rest of the group and approached his car. Winding down his window, he looked at the teenager and suddenly realised why he felt the way he did. It was Tom Carter, his brother's best mate. What the fuck was he doing here? He hadn't seen or heard anything about Tom since he had run away from home four or five years ago.

At the same time he recognised Tom, Tom recognised him, gasped

Take a Chance

and looked at him in horror. Seb watched him shake his head and back away from the car. Seb opened the door and shouted, "Tom!" Tom continued shaking his head, then spun on his heel and ran away.

Chapter Four

Oh fuck, oh fuck, oh fuck!

What the fuck was Seb doing in this part of Manchester? Fuck, he'd recognised him too. Tom was going to be sick, and he swallowed continuously as saliva flooded his mouth and his stomach churned. As he ran, he kept looking over his shoulder to check Seb wasn't following him. He crossed to the other side of the street, and trying to catch his breath, slowed to a walk.

It had easily been four years since he'd last seen Seb, but he had recognised him instantly. He groaned at the thought of Seb seeing him and knowing what he was doing. A car pulled up in front of him and for a moment, he thought it was Seb but realised the car was the wrong colour. This one was a red BMW.

The window was down, and a heavyset man with red hair asked, "How much?"

Looking down the street, Tom replied, "Er, fifty quid?" He rubbed the back of his neck as he spoke.

"Okay, where?"

"See that alley just there--" Tom pointed to one about twenty metres away-- "pull in there."

Tom watched as the car drove away. It pulled into the alley he'd pointed out and waited. Looking over his shoulder, Tom walked over to the car and got in.

"Money first," Tom stated.

"Sure."

Tom watched as the bloke counted out the money and handed it over. He got out of the front of the car and into the back. Taking a condom out of his rear pocket, Tom handed it over then pulled his jeans down. He watched as the punter ripped open the foil packet, took out the condom and rolled it on. Tom swallowed as acid burned in his stomach and up his throat. He shouldn't be doing this, not right now, not after what had just happened.

Just when Tom decided to tell the bloke that this was a mistake, the punter growled, "Bend over the back seat."

Taking a deep breath and trying to detach himself from what was about to happen, he bent over the seat and was grabbed roughly from behind, with one hand in his hair and the other on his hip. Turning to look over his shoulder, he said, "Hey, not so rough."

"I paid for a fuck, so we'll do it anyway I want."

Tom felt him start to push his cock in between his arse cheeks and gritted his teeth. He tried to relax and push out but couldn't, and it felt like he was being torn apart as the man pushed in past the muscle. Fuck, it hurt! Tom gripped the seat with his hands and bit his lip to stop crying out. The punter didn't stop until he was fully in and immediately started to fuck him hard. The punter slammed into Tom, and he grunted from the force of the thrusts as he screwed his eyes shut and tried to ignore what was happening to him. He felt the hand holding his hip move to his shoulder and pull him back as the guy fucked him. Tom felt his hair being pulled and was again forced to grit his teeth. Tom's head was pulled back, and his scalp screamed in protest at the rough treatment. Again, he was forced to bite his lip, and he knew he was going to be in pain after this.

After what felt like an hour but was only a couple of minutes, the movements behind him become more erratic as the punter began to orgasm. Suddenly, he heard a loud groan from behind him as the punter tensed up, followed by heavy breathing. He felt him pull out and winced at the sudden flare of pain. He immediately started to get dressed. As Tom was pulling his jeans up, he was pushed out of the car door and landed hard on the road, the gravel digging painfully into his hip and thigh. The punter threw the used condom in his face, slamming the car door shut. Tom quickly pulled it off and threw it on the floor. He looked up angrily at the car, but the engine started and pulled away quickly, drowning out anything he was going to say.

Tom groaned as he slowly stood up and gently tried to remove the bits of gravel from his hip and thigh but could already see blood from some of the scrapes left behind. Pulling his jeans up, he began to walk back to the street. As he walked, he winced and gasped at the pain that radiated around his groin and arse. His hip, thigh and arse hurt to the point where he had to limp to try and alleviate it. Now that it was over, all he could do was shake his head at his own stupidity. His stomach churned, and he swallowed the saliva that suddenly pooled in his mouth. Breathing deeply, he tried to control his emotions.

He'd been an idiot. They worked together for a reason, and he had run off, then got into a car with no one around to take any details of the vehicle. Shit, he could've ended up like Adam or worse. Tom smacked himself on the head and immediately regretted it as the pain seemed to increase everywhere else.

Take a Chance

It took Tom almost thirty minutes to make the slow walk back to the house, and he found it empty when he walked in which he was grateful for. He didn't want to answer any questions about tonight and what had happened. He made his way upstairs and stripped in the bathroom. There was no electricity for light, so he couldn't see the extent of his injuries but cleaned up as best as he could with cold water, shivering as he did.

He gently touched himself and winced at the flare of pain. He could tell he had a tear and knew he would have to let it heal, otherwise he would be risking further damage and then possible infection. He lowered his head onto the sink and felt the cold from it seep through his skin as he inhaled shakily. He kept breathing slowly in an attempt to calm his rapidly beating heart. He'd been stupid. Anything could have happened to him.

Tom limped into the bedroom and crawled into his sleeping bag, curling up on his side. Never had he felt as alone as he did right at that moment. Seeing Seb had brought back painful memories of how he'd ended up on the streets. He honestly hadn't thought his parents would throw him out for being gay. He'd heard and read about those things happening to other people, but he never thought he would be one of them. Then to have his supposed best mate and his parents shut the door in his face without a word had been even worse. Tom snorted. So being gay was worse than getting some girl pregnant. That's what he had been accused of by his parents that night and how he had ended up telling them the truth about his sexuality.

He could still remember that night so clearly. He'd walked the streets for hours, crying, wondering what he was going to do. He'd been so frightened as he was only fifteen at the time. Who kicked a fifteen-year-old out for being gay? He only had the clothes he was wearing and some pocket money. He'd ended up spending the night in a garden shed someone had left unlocked.

After a freezing, sleepless night spent on the shed floor, crying, he'd gone back home to see if he could work things out with his parents. When he had gotten there, he'd noticed that their car was gone and had decided to go in and wait for them. He'd tried his key in the front door, but it wouldn't turn. His heart had started beating faster when he'd realised that they had changed the locks after they'd thrown him out. He'd climbed over the gate and had tried the back door, but the same thing had happened. He couldn't remember how long he had stood there for, frozen with the realisation that his parents had not only thrown him out but had changed the locks to stop him from getting back in. Furious, he had picked up a rock from the garden and thrown it at the window.

Looking around his room, he groaned aloud. Now Seb knew what he did. God, what must he be thinking? Or did he think he deserved it too? It didn't help that he was even better looking than he remembered. Man, he had one major crush on him when he was younger. He'd even had fantasies of them being together. Sweet, pathetic dreams. Dreams that would never, in reality, occur. He wrapped his arms around his legs and breathed raggedly. As he continued to think about his past, Tom felt the first tears start to fall and did nothing to stop them.

All the next day, Seb thought about Tom. He'd been distracted the night before to the point where he'd made excuses and had left his friend's house early, which was unusual for him, especially as he was celebrating.

As it was getting closer to Christmas, he'd arranged to meet one of his co-workers in Manchester City centre to do some Christmas shopping, but again found himself constantly thinking about Tom. He knew the area he had seen him in, knew what went on there but couldn't bring himself to believe that he had seen Tom doing that.

It had easily been four or five years since he had last seen Tom, a time when he had come home from University, and Tom had been hanging around with Josh. Tom and Josh had been inseparable since they had started high school together. He'd heard from his parents what had happened and why Tom had left home. They had all been friends and apparently Tom had gotten one the girls pregnant. Liz, was it? He couldn't quite remember, and rather than face up to his responsibilities, Tom had left.

And now he was selling himself.

"Hello, Earth to Seb!"

Seb looked up at Dave and smiled. "Sorry, mate, I was miles away."

"Yeah, I noticed, especially when I started talking about the stripper I took home last night that both me and the wife banged."

"Huh, what?" What was he talking about?

Dave laughed and shook his head. "Exactly. What has you thinking so hard?"

Seb frowned and sighed deeply. "I saw someone last night, and it just surprised me is all." He shrugged before continuing, "Surprised."

"Want to share?"

Really? Er no. "Nah, I'll figure it out, and anyway, we need to get this shopping done. I'm not going through last minute hell like last year. I've still got heel impressions on my back."

Dave grimaced. "Yeah, maybe you're right. Come on then, let's get to it. The sooner we get started, the sooner we can leave."

They both stood and left the restaurant they'd stopped for lunch in and walked towards the Arndale Centre. It was hell. Seb hated shopping at the best of times but with it being the lead-up to Christmas, which was still a month away, places were starting to get busier than usual. He couldn't wait for it to be over. If it was like this in November, what would it be like Christmas Eve?

He spent the rest of the afternoon in shopping hell before deciding he'd had enough and said goodbye to Dave, then headed home. When he arrived home, he unpacked all his bags and decided there was no way in hell he was doing that again, and if he had forgotten any presents, it was tough. He wasn't going back.

He switched on the TV and threw himself on the sofa, but again found himself thinking of Tom. He had looked a mess. Skinny, almost gaunt, with dark circles under his eyes and he'd had on dirty, threadbare clothes for this time of year and they looked like they would fall apart in a spin cycle. How long had he been wearing them? Where was he living? Could he even afford to live somewhere or was he out on the streets? Shit, was he an alcoholic or taking drugs? Was that why he had become a rent boy? Letting strangers fuck him for money, so he could buy drugs or booze?

Seb didn't like to think of Tom doing that, but it had been unmistakable, and it made him want to throw up, knowing that he had to sell himself for money and food. To stay alive. Why hadn't he just accepted his responsibilities and manned up?

All Seb had was a lot of questions and no answers whatsoever. Even so, he wanted answers because he still thought of Tom as a sort of friend and couldn't stand by and not try to help him.

Seb mulled over what he was going to do while he made and drank his tea. When nine o'clock came, he got his wallet, car keys, coat and left.

❊❊❊

Take a Chance

After a night spent tossing and turning with very little sleep, Tom had spent most of the day sat in the lounge, not paying attention to anyone or joining in the conversations taking place around him. His arse spasmed, causing him to wince, and his stomach turned over, firstly, over what he'd done in that alley and secondly, for seeing Seb.

Banging his head against the wall he leaned on, Tom closed his eyes and sighed deeply. His life was fucked up. What he wouldn't give to be able to walk away and start all over again. To actually live rather than exist as he was doing.

He opened his eyes and glanced at the others in the room and sighed again. Dropping his gaze to the floor, he played with the dirt that was on it and thought about his options. Leaving these guys on their own wasn't one of them. He knew he wasn't responsible for them, but they were his family and with them being younger than he was, he wanted to watch out for them. He wanted to make sure they didn't make the same mistakes he'd made. He hadn't had anyone looking out for him when he had found himself on the streets, and he cringed at some of the things he'd done before realising how things worked.

Glancing out of the window, Tom could see it was dark outside, so he knew it was evening. The sun set earlier in winter so it was hard to tell the exact time and he didn't have a watch or clock, so it was all guesswork.

Deciding he needed to get out, he stood up and grabbed his coat. "I'm heading out," he told no one in particular as he left the room. He heard the replies as he walked out but paid no attention to them. He let himself out of the house and slowly strolled to the coffee shop he liked to visit.

Tom entered the coffee shop and bought the cheapest drink they had to offer. Sam wasn't working, so he didn't stop to chat and, to be honest, he wasn't in the mood for talking. He took his drink and sat at a table by the window, wincing as he did, before staring at the reflection of himself. He looked older than what he was, but this type of life would do that for you when you were living day to day. He supposed he was luckier than some; living as he did with the others meant they watched out for each other and, occasionally, when possible, helped each other out. They were all in the same situation; no money, no home, but somehow they made it work. Lost in his thoughts, he hadn't realised that it was closing time until he heard someone come over and speak to him.

"Hey, just to let you know, we're closing soon."

Tom looked up in surprise. "Oh, okay. Thanks."

Tom stood and smiled as he passed his empty cup over and made his way out of the coffee shop.

He walked down the street, head down against the cold, which caused him to shiver and pull his thin coat tighter around him. As he wasn't paying attention, he almost walked into someone. Not bothering to look up, he muttered an apology and carried on, keeping his head down and hoping not to draw any unwanted attention.

"That's alright, Tom. It's you I've come to see."

Tom looked up to see Seb stood in front of him.

Chapter Five

Seb smiled shyly at Tom. "I thought it was you I saw last night. How are you?" he asked.

"What do you want, Seb?" Tom asked bouncing on the balls of his feet.

Seb shrugged. "I thought I would find you and see how you are."

"How I am?" Tom asked as he frowned, tilting his head to the side.

"Er, yeah, I've not seen you in years, so I thought...Yeah. I thought I'd say hi."

Tom stood there, shaking his head slowly, not quite taking in what Seb was saying. He had nothing to say to Seb. Not now. Not ever.

"Wow, this is much more awkward than I thought it would be," Seb commented with an awkward laugh as he rubbed the back of his neck. "Want to get a drink with me? Catch up?"

"Catch up?" Why the fuck would he want to catch up?

Seb smiled. "Yeah, catch up, have a drink together, talk. If you want to."

Tom shook his head at him. "I've got nothing to fuckin' say to you."

"What d'you mean? We used to talk all the time. We've known each other for years."

"Really?" Tom huffed out a shallow laugh.

"Yeah, really." Seb sighed. "I looked for you when you left. Couldn't believe you'd walk away like that. I was worried, but I couldn't find you anywhere."

Tom stared at him, stunned. Walk away! What the fuck! "Walk away? I didn't walk away. I was thrown out! Oh yeah, and I came to yours, and your fuckin' parents shut the door in my fuckin' face with Josh staring at me from the window."

Seb looked shocked, eyes wide, mouth dropping open. "You came to mine? I didn't know that."

"Of course I did. Where else would I go but to my best mate? I had nothing!" Tom turned around frustrated. All this had happened years ago, and he just wanted to forget it. He turned back to Seb. "Why are you here? I mean really?" he asked.

Seb stared intently at him looking like he was debating what he was going to say. "You're selling yourself." It was a statement, not a question.

Tom glared at Seb, not sure how to answer. It was obvious what he'd been doing, given where he was when Seb had seen him, and Seb wasn't an idiot. "Yeah," he answered honestly waiting for Seb's reaction.

Seb looked surprised that he had answered him truthfully. "Why? You're so much better than that."

Take a Chance

"How the fuck would you know? Huh. Are you judging me? Don't you stand there and fuckin' judge me," his voice shaking with fury, "don't you fuckin' dare." Tom pointed his finger at Seb's chest as he spoke.

Seb held his hands up in a passive gesture while shaking his head. "I'm not judging you, honestly. Just, please explain it to me."

Tom shook his head and turned as he walked away. "It was nice to see you again. Seb, nice catching up," he grunted sarcastically. "I'll see you around."

"No, wait, please, Tom," Seb pleaded. "I'm sorry if I've upset you." He grabbed his hair in frustration. "Why couldn't you have stayed? I know you were young, but surely being a dad would have been better than this?"

Tom gaped at him. What the fuck had he just said to him? He turned abruptly from him again and strode away quickly. "Fuck you," he shouted over his shoulder as Seb ran after him, grabbing his arm and spinning him around.

"Don't walk away from me. Explain it to me. We're supposed to be friends."

"I'm not explainin' shit to you," Tom snapped as he snatched his arm away. "Think what you want. Hey, I'll tell you what. Why don't you go and talk to mummy and daddy and Josh why they wouldn't help me and leave me the fuck alone."

Tom walked off again, and this time, Seb let him go. He was angry and frustrated that the lies from his past were being dragged up. Stopping at an off-license, he bought a cheap bottle of cider and went home with it, planning to drink until he forgot about it all.

Why did Seb have to see him? Why did he have to look for him? And why did he have to dredge it all up again? Oh yeah and why, after all this time, was he still being blamed for getting Liz pregnant? Surely coming out as gay would have made people realise he couldn't have been the father?

Maybe his parents had kept quiet about that. Tom snorted. Of course, they would. They couldn't have people knowing they had a gay son. Not good for the image they tried so hard to maintain. Where is it that having a son run off because he got someone pregnant was better than admitting their son was gay? How fucked up was that?

Tom walked back into the house and wasn't surprised to find it empty. The others were probably out working, which if he were honest, he should have been doing, even if he was still sore from the night before. But, he just couldn't face doing it, and that feeling had been growing stronger with each passing day.

What did it matter what he wanted? This life was all he had; it was all he knew. He had no education, and he had no family. But, how much longer could he continue to do this for?

Stuck, that was how Tom felt. Trapped in a hole with no way out. No wonder so many others drank or did drugs. To block out the shame, the misery and helplessness they felt. Tom just felt used, soiled, like a piece of meat. It didn't matter how much he scrubbed himself; he could never get clean. All he could see was the dirt that covered him.

Looking around the lounge, he sat in the corner and opened the bottle of cider. He stared at it, feeling the cold and condensation on his hand from the bottle wondering why he wasn't one of those people who could drown out their shit lives with alcohol or drugs. Make it all go away. Lifting it to his lips, he took a long drink, then another and another. Putting the bottle down carefully, Tom hung his head and rocked himself.

When Tom woke up the next morning, he had the hangover from Hell. His head pounded, the room spun and his mouth tasted like something had crawled in it and died. And his stomach? It was trying

Take a Chance

to make a break for freedom. He swallowed as his mouth flooded with saliva and tried to stop himself from being sick.

He sat up and instantly wished he hadn't. The spinning was so much worse now, and his stomach contents were attempting to erupt out of his mouth, throat burning as bile came up. Tom lay back down slowly and curled up on his side. He screwed his eyes tightly shut praying his stomach would settle; he didn't think he would make it to a sink or the garden if he had to move suddenly. He looked around until he found the now empty bottle of cider and grimaced. No wonder he felt like shit. Closing his eyes, he hoped that he would fall asleep, and this feeling would disappear. He was never drinking again. No. Not a single drop.

Seb pulled up outside his parents' house and turned the engine off. He sat staring at the front of the house and wondered how he was going to approach the subject of Tom. He'd seemed surprised that Seb thought he'd gotten that girl pregnant. He knew his parents and Josh hadn't mentioned Tom since he had left home, but according to him, he'd come here asking for help. Considering how close Josh had been to Tom, it surprised him that Josh never once made any comment regarding him after he had left. But he hadn't asked either, had he? So, was he just as guilty?

Sighing, Seb leaned his head back against the car seat and closed his eyes. He couldn't get the image of Tom out of his mind and what he had to do to live or the fact that he still found Tom attractive. It didn't matter that he knew what Tom did, he was still drawn to him.

With that thought, he opened the door and got out of his car, closing it behind him. He walked up the driveway to his parents, pulling his keys out as he got near the front door and letting himself in. "Hi Mum, Dad. It's me," he called as he walked in.

His mum, Kath, walked into the hallway and smiled as she hugged him. "You're just in time. I'm setting the table now. Why don't you tell your dad it's ready and to come through. He's watching the football in the living room."

"Alright, Mum."

Seb walked into the living room to find his dad sat watching football on the TV. "How are they doing, Dad?"

His dad grunted, "Not bloody well. Pay all that money in wages and I could play better than them. It's Man United!"

"Well, Everton aren't that bad, you know."

"But it's United! They should be all over them."

Seb hid a smile as he watched his dad get more and more frustrated with the game. "Come on, Dad. Mum said lunch is ready, and I'm starving."

"Bloody woman! The match is on," his dad grumbled while standing and switching off the TV.

"I heard that, John! Get in here and carve the meat," his mum shouted from the kitchen.

Seb laughed. "Busted."

"Yeah, but she loves me." John chuckled.

They entered the dining room just as his mum walked in with the meat. The table had already been set, and the plates had the vegetables on them. The smell was delicious. Seb's stomach rumbled as he sat down and looked at the food. His mum made the best Sunday roast. He watched his dad carve the meat and put several slices on Seb's plate.

Once everyone had sat, his parents asked him about his job and the contract, and he spent several minutes explaining everything to them. Nothing had changed, but the security of having a full-time job did take the pressure and worry off of him.

When his dad finished chewing, he asked Seb. "Where were you Friday night? I called, but there was no answer."

"Yeah, I went out to celebrate with some mates, which reminds me. You won't believe who I saw while I was out. Tom." He paused and then asked, "You remember him, don't you? Josh's mate."

When no one replied, Seb looked up from his plate and frowned when he saw both parents staring at him.

"What?" Seb asked, frowning at his parents.

"You saw Tom?" his Mum questioned him.

"Yeah. Don't you think it was strange the way he left? Why did he leave home at such a young age?"

His mum made a strangled noise, and her face looked pinched. "No. He got what he deserved, the dirty, disease-riddled fag!"

Seb's mouth dropped open. What? Had she really just said that? Dirty, disease-riddled fag? He knew they didn't like gay people, but this?

"Your mum is right, Sebastian. You don't want his type hanging around," Seb's dad agreed.

"I'm sorry, did you just say dirty, disease-riddled fag? You're telling me he's gay? I thought he got that girl, Liz, pregnant and that's why he left home."

His mum shook her head. "No, he admitted he was a fag to his parents, and that he wasn't the father because of it. He left them no choice. Good Catholic people. They couldn't have him living there defiling their home with his lifestyle. They were so ashamed that their son was gay! They made the right decision by having him leave and then to think he came around here and asked us for help! Like we would help his type of scum. He's better off dead, and I hope he burns in Hell! It's a sin what he is. It says so in the Bible."

His dad nodded his head in agreement. "We don't want any fairy near us, do we, Kath? God knows what you can catch from their like. We firmly believe their kind should be castrated. At least then parents would know that their children are safe. And don't even get me started on them adopting children. It would be giving them a license to abuse them."

Seb spluttered, "Their like? Fairy? Children being safe? You know it's OK to be gay, right? You know gay men aren't paedophiles?"

His mum leaned forward and banged her fist on the table. "No, it's not alright. Not at all. It's a sin according to God, and we don't want his kind dirtying everything that's good in this world. I'm telling you now, Sebastian, don't speak to him again. He's a deviant and will go to Hell. You mark my words. I was hoping he would be dead by now, but I guess he couldn't even do that right."

Seb sat back in his chair stunned by what he was hearing from his parents. Yeah, he knew they were religious, but this? When had they become like this, so bigoted? When had they started spewing this hatred? Castration? What the fuck!

His dad looked at him frowning, mouth tight from across the table and pointed his finger at him. "You listen to me, son. I'll only say this once. Being gay is a sin in the eyes of Our Lord, and I will not tolerate you being friends with the likes of him. He got everything he deserved. To do those things to other men is sick and twisted and perverted. They should all be taken out and shot. It would make the world a better place. Some of these foreign countries have the right idea by banning it and making it a crime. I only wish we would do it here. The country would be a nicer place to live. We wouldn't have to witness their kind holding hands or kissing in public."

Take a Chance

Seb's mouth hung open, and he struggled to breathe. He was shocked at what they were saying to him. Sick, twisted, perverted? Did he really hear his dad say those things? Sure, he'd heard his parents make the odd comment here and there, but this level of hatred was staggering. It went beyond anything he would have ever thought he would hear his parents say.

His mum looked at him as she picked up her cutlery and started to eat again. "Now let's forget about that nasty business and finish our meal. I've got apple crumble and custard for desert. Baked it this morning. Now tell me, when are you going to bring a nice young lady home for us to meet? It's about time you did. You're not getting any younger, you know."

Seb sat for another minute staring at his parents before he did as they had asked him. He made polite conversation with them, but it was a struggle, his stomach rolling and churning. He could barely swallow the food, worried he'd bring it back up. Would they be like that with him?

Now he knew he'd made the right choice by not telling them he liked men as well as women. He didn't want to be around them. He couldn't wait to finish so he could make his excuses and leave.

Megs Pritchard

Chapter Six

After what felt like hours later, Tom dragged himself out of bed and gingerly made his way to the bathroom, holding his churning stomach. He couldn't remember coming upstairs; he'd been that drunk. The room had now stopped spinning, thankfully, but his head was pounding in time to his pulse. His mouth was a cesspool, and his breath could kill the living from fifty feet away. He spent a few minutes in the bathroom washing and trying to eradicate the decaying corpses that had taken up residence in his mouth before going downstairs.

He needed coffee and lots of it, and he desperately wanted a greasy fry up even though his stomach still wasn't quite on board with that idea. He knew he had to be careful with his money, but at the moment, he didn't give a shit. If he needed to, he would go out that night. What was one more night anyway?

He left the house without stopping to talk to anyone; he just didn't have anything to say. He walked towards this little greasy spoon cafe he knew did all day breakfast fairly cheap.

He wasn't paying much attention to where he was walking, probably because the light stung his eyes when he did, so he didn't notice when a car pulled up in front of him. It was only when he heard his name shouted that he looked up and saw the car, recognising it as the one Seb had driven and started to walk faster as he swore. What did he want now? Hadn't he said everything last night to him?

"Tom, wait! Please don't walk away. I want to talk to you, to apologise." Seb stood in front of him, his hands held out in front of him. "Let me buy you a drink or something, and we can talk."

"Why? There's nothing more to say."

"Please, Tom. I know alright. I spoke to my parents today, and they told me why you left home, you know, for being gay." Seb ran his hand through his hair. "Fuck, I also know my family did nothing to help you, and I'm sorry. You should never have been treated like that."

"So what, you decided to buy me a drink to make it up to me for having shitty friends and a shittier family?" Tom scowled at him.

"I don't want to upset you, Tom. I just want to have a drink with someone I haven't seen in years. Someone I was worried about and now have the chance to know again. Please."

Tom looked at him for a minute, then sighed and dropped his shoulders. What did it matter if he let Seb buy him a drink? He'd leave soon enough, and he'd be back to where he was before. A few minutes now wouldn't change anything.

Tom nodded his head and pointed up the road. "I'm goin' to the café down the road to get something to eat. They do all day breakfasts."

"Alright then."

Tom started walking towards the café, and Seb followed him, both of them silent. He glanced at Seb, trying to gauge what he could be thinking or feeling, but his face was blank.

Tom stopped outside the cafe and looked at Seb. "Well, here it is." Seb looked up at him, surprise showing on his face as his eyes widened slightly.

"Oh, I didn't think we were this close." They stood looking at each other awkwardly. "Er... should we go in then?" Seb asked.

Tom nodded and opened the door, stepping inside. Seb followed him and looked around. The coffee shop had off white walls with a couple of pictures hanging and boards advertising what they served and the cost. Nothing fancy but the smells were wonderful.

"Sit down, Tom, I'll order. What do you want?" Seb asked him.

Tom looked at him and reached into his back pocket pulling some money out. "I can pay for my own fuckin' food," he grunted. Seb wasn't going to pay for him.

"I know, but I offered, so I'm going to pay. I ate earlier, so I'm just having a coffee. You mentioned something about breakfast. Is that what you want?"

Tom stared at him while deciding if he should take him up on his offer. Why the fuck not? He nodded. "Yeah, thanks. The full English please and a coffee."

Tom walked over to a table by the window and sat staring out, watching people walk past. Had he done the right thing by agreeing to come here with Seb? Or, had he made a mistake? It was clear Seb wanted to talk to him. It was the second time Seb had hunted him down, but Tom was unsure why he had. What more could they possibly say to each other? He ran his fingers over the top of the table, feeling the scuffs and scratches on its surface. Why had he agreed? What could they have to talk about?

Take a Chance

Sighing, Tom turned to watch Seb as he placed their order. Tom had always found Seb attractive but with Tom being Josh's best mate and Seb Josh's brother meant he couldn't entertain the possibility of trying anything with him. Oh, and the fact that Seb had a girlfriend the last time he had seen him. It wasn't a great idea liking the straight guy who just happened to be your best mate's brother.

Now that Seb was older, he was better looking, with his black hair and hazel eyes. Taller than Tom, but Tom didn't know how tall he was. Tom clenched his fists as he watched him. What he wouldn't give to have the life Seb had.

He watched as Seb paid, then made his way over to the table before sitting down opposite him. They sat glancing at each other for several uncomfortable minutes before Seb finally sighed and asked, "How was your night?"

"Are you asking me did I get fucked?" Tom replied sarcastically.

Seb sat back and stared at him as he shook his head. "No, no, that's not why I'm asking at all. I'm just trying to make conversation."

"Well, after seeing you, I went home and got so pissed that I passed out on the floor. Great night."

"Alright, that explains the need for greasy food and coffee." Seb took a deep breath and exhaled loudly as he rubbed his head. "Look, I don't want to argue with you, okay? I don't know...I just," he sighed before continuing, "I spoke to my parents today, asked about you. I know I was wrong about why you left home, and I'm sorry. I was told you were the father, and you had run because you didn't want the responsibility. No one ever mentioned that you'd come out and had left home."

"I didn't leave home. I told you that." Tom spoke through clenched teeth as he gave Seb a hard stare.

Seb nodded and sighed again. "Yeah, you did. Sorry."

Tom didn't reply, and an awkward silence developed between them. "How's Josh?" Tom suddenly asked, changing the subject.

Seb looked confused for a second at the change in the conversation but then grunted before answering. "Failing by the sounds of it."

"He's at Uni then?"

Seb nodded. "Yeah, not studying though. My parents are a little disappointed in him. They're paying his fees, and he doesn't even go to class."

Tom snorted. "Nothing's changed there then."

"What do you mean? He did alright at school."

"Did he? I guess that was 'cause his mates were helping him out. He was like that at school. Got his mates to pull his arse out of the shit before he got expelled. You didn't know?"

Seb sighed and slowly shook his head. "No, I'd just started my second year at Uni when you guys started your final year at school. I wasn't around as often."

"So I guess you know what it's like."

"I was never that bad."

"Really?" Tom smiled before continuing, "I'd have thought that was what all students did. Drink, drugs, fuckin'." Tom shrugged. "Well, I guess it is for Josh."

Seb cleared his throat. "Look, I know you don't want to talk about it, but can you tell me what actually happened? I've heard different things and some of the things my parents said... well, they weren't great."

"You're fuckin' right. I don't--"

They were interrupted by the food arriving, and Tom started eating immediately, even though he wasn't hungry anymore and the food was hot. He barely tasted the food, and his stomach had a lead weight in it. He didn't want to talk about what had happened even if Seb knew some of the truth now. He just wanted to forget all about it and try to get on with his life, however shitty it was.

They sat in silence while he ate with Tom doing the best he could to ignore Seb completely, but it was hard with him sitting opposite and sighing occasionally. He finished his food in record time and drank his coffee. Standing up, he looked at Seb. "Thanks for the food," he muttered before walking to the door.

Tom heard the chair scrape on the floor behind him and knew Seb was getting up to follow him out. "Hey, hold up, Tom. Can't we talk?"

Tom turned to face Seb once he was outside, pissed off. "What about, Seb? What could we possibly have to talk to each other about? Want to know how much I charge for a blow job or a fuck? Are you interested?"

"I'm not interested in any of that. Stop treating me like some fucking piece of shit. Like what happened to you is somehow my fault. I'm trying here. Do you know how I felt when I realised someone I knew was a fucking rent boy?" Seb paused, gripping the back of his neck. "You might not have considered us friends, but I did. I want to help you, alright. I still consider you my friend, regardless of how you feel about it. And yeah, I feel like shit thinking about what you have to do to stay alive, and I fucking hate it. It makes me sick to think of you having to do those things.

"I don't know what happened between you and your parents, okay? I don't know why they would throw you out for being gay, but I'm still here and I'm still your friend."

Tom shook his head, glaring at Seb. "You don't get it, do you? I don't want a fuckin' friend, and if I did, I certainly wouldn't choose you. Just fuck off and leave me alone."

Tom turned and walked away, leaving Seb standing there watching him. What he wouldn't give to be able to believe what Seb had said. But who would want to be his friend? Hadn't everyone he'd ever trusted and loved turned their backs on him when he needed them the most? No, it was best just to forget all about Seb and his claims of wanting to be his friend. It wouldn't hurt as much when Seb would have eventually walked out of his life.

※ ※ ※

Seb watched Tom walk away and grabbed his hair in frustration. Should he follow him or let him go? They would probably only argue more, and clearly, Tom didn't want to talk to him about anything that had happened in the past. Yeah, he was pissed at how Tom had reacted, and he should walk away and forget about him, but he found that he couldn't. He couldn't be like Tom's parents. He couldn't be like his parents, and he certainly couldn't be like Josh. He understood Tom being angry and lashing out at him. He was a reminder of his past, and he obviously didn't want to remember it.

He sighed and walked back to where he'd parked his car, getting in and starting it. He sat there watching Tom as he virtually ran away from him. He closed his eyes, leaning back in his seat. He would have to give it some time, let things settle between them before he tried to speak to him again. Given how angry Tom was right now, they'd get nowhere and would no doubt end up arguing again, which would accomplish nothing. Sighing again, Seb slowly drove away.

As he walked into his house, his phone rang. Without looking at the screen, Seb answered. "Hello."

"Hey, Seb. Not heard from you in a couple of days. How are you?" It was Finley, a close friend from Uni. Someone he could talk to who wouldn't judge him or Tom.

Sighing, Seb slumped on the sofa. "It's been a shit couple of days."

"Why? What's up?"

Seb told Finley about seeing Tom and everything that had occurred since. "I'm not sure what to do. Do I just forget about seeing him?"

There was silence on the phone for a few seconds before Finley spoke. "I don't know, Seb. That shit's fucked up. How would you feel about forgetting you ever saw him?"

Seb inhaled sharply. The thought of leaving Tom like that sickened him. "I...I...no. I don't think I could."

"Then that's your answer, isn't it?"

"Yes, I guess it is."

"Let me know, one way or the other."

"I will and, thanks, Fin. I appreciate it."

"Speak to you later."

Seb hung up, placing the phone next to him on the sofa. He had a lot to think about.

※ ※ ※

The week passed quickly for Seb, with new cases to start looking into and more responsibilities to take on. Even though it was technically the same job, he felt more pressure to prove he could justify the contract. At the end of each day, he'd fallen into bed tired from all the processing of information he'd been doing. And yet, he'd thought about Tom constantly. Was he hooking? Was he being safe and using condoms? Did he have enough money to eat? He looked so thin and his clothes couldn't hide that fact.

Whenever he thought of what Tom might be doing, his stomach lurched violently, and he had to close his eyes and breathe deeply to avoid vomiting. The thought of Tom being used as a quick fuck. Maybe some guys get off on the anonymous sex thing, but then they could just go to a club and get it free, so why pay? Maybe it was married men who did it? Maybe it was the idea of paying for it? He didn't know, and to be honest, he didn't want to know. But he couldn't help picturing all the things that could happen to Tom. And if he was honest, a small part of him wanted to be doing certain things to Tom as well. Not the paying for it and doing it in some alley or back seat somewhere, but the holding and loving him part and showing him that it didn't have to be that way.

When it was Friday night, Seb knew he was going to go looking for Tom again and try to talk to him, to see if they could somehow form a tentative friendship. When he arrived home from work, he changed clothes and waited until it was later in the evening before he left to go out searching for Tom.

Take a Chance

Chapter Seven

It was Friday and Tom, Matt and Luke were discussing which area to work in that night. It was always busy around the city centre and the gay village, so they had a multitude of areas to choose from. The weather had been shit all week, so there hadn't been much work, and there was hardly any food or money left. Once they'd decided where they were going, they started to get ready.

Tom knew their group did better than most. Most people who lived on the streets didn't have two pennies to rub together. But most people on the streets were feeding some form of addiction.

Fortunately, Tom had managed to avoid falling into that trap, but he'd seen plenty of others who hadn't been so lucky. He understood why others succumbed to drug or alcohol abuse. It helped you escape this so called life for a short while.

Tom turned to see Ben and Adam in the doorway. "Hey, you guys goin' out tonight?"

"Yeah, need the money," Ben answered.

Tom nodded. "Same here. Are you goin' your usual place?"

"Yeah, so I guess we'll see you out there."

"Yeah okay. Be safe out there, they still haven't found those two blokes yet."

Ben nodded, but Adam didn't respond, just stood staring at Tom making him feel like he was under a microscope. Tom watched as they both left. He shook his head before he turned to face Luke and Matt and smiled. "Ready to go?"

"Yeah," Matt answered as he ran his fingers through his brown hair, trying to style it. "Usual place?"

"Yeah. Be safe, you two and I'll see ya later." Tom left the house and headed towards Canal Street as he wrapped his thin coat around him to try and keep warm. Goosebumps popped up on his skin and he shivered in the cold air. It was busy when he got there, which wasn't surprising as it was Friday night. Since *Queer as Folk* had been on TV, Canal Street had become a hub for the gay community outside of London, so there was always something going on and the area drew large groups.

Dodging a group of people who were already drunk, as they stumbled out of Via, Tom continued towards the end of Canal Street before heading towards Piccadilly Gardens. Not the safest of areas but one he knew well, and he knew the people who worked there both male and female.

As he was walking along, a car pulled up beside him. Tom turned towards the car and plastered a fake smile on his face as he walked over to the window. Leaning over, he saw who it was. "For fuck's sake!" he muttered. "What do you want?" he asked as he pushed away from the car.

Seb parked up and got out, leaving the door open. "What? You working?"

"Actually, yeah I am, and you're scaring away all the punters, so fuck off!"

Seb grabbed him and shouted, "No, I won't." He took a deep breath. "I won't let you walk away again. I want to help. I'm not like your parents, and it doesn't have to be like this. You don't have to sell yourself. I don't know what it's been like for you, but there has to be something better than this."

What. The. Fuck! "No, you don't know what it's been like for me!" screamed Tom. "My parents, they threw me out like yesterday's rubbish, they didn't give a shit. I was fifteen, man, how the hell was I supposed to look after myself? There's nothing better for someone like me, so just leave me the fuck alone!"

"No, I can't just walk away knowing what you're doing. Explain it to me. Why this, Tom? Why turn to this?" Seb asked him with genuine interest shining from his brown eyes.

Tom spun away from Seb, looking at his feet while running his hands through his hair, as he paced back and forth in front of him. Talking about his choice to sell himself wasn't a conversation he wanted to be having, but fuck, he'd made the best he could with what he had, which was nothing. He turned back to Seb as he looked up into the night sky. Closing his eyes, Tom inhaled deeply, holding the air in his lungs. How could he explain why he had resorted to selling himself? What could he say?

Tom glanced at Seb and exhaled. "I know this isn't what you wanted to hear, your brother's mate, the rent boy, the whore, taking money for blow jobs or back alley fucks." Tom paused and looked at Seb. "I look in the mirror and see who I am, what I've become to pay for food, the occasional roof over my head. I wish things could have been different. I wish they'd accepted me for who I am." Tom shrugged. "I should have known they'd never accept their son as gay." Tom laughed bitterly. "Do you know they never even let me get my stuff from my room? I left with the clothes on my back and money from my Saturday job. That was it. That first night on the streets, I didn't know who to turn to or where to go." Tom shook his head. "Do you think I want to be gay? Do you think I would choose this life?"

"Tom, I'm--"

"Save it, Seb. Whatever you're gonna say, don't," Tom muttered quietly. "Look, I can't stay here, I have to go."

Tom turned to walk away when Seb grabbed him by the arm and pulled him around to face him. "You think I'm judging you for the choices you've made? Fuck, I don't know what I would've done in your place. I can't stand here and say I'm happy with you being fucked for money. I just don't know why you never came to me or tried to contact me. I was your friend too, Tom. You could've come to me. Honestly? I feel sick that you had to do this, but you're here now, and I can't let you leave. I can't let you carry on doing what you're doing." Seb stood and held out his hand to Tom. "Come back to mine tonight. We can talk some more."

Tom shook his head. "I can't."

"Why? What's keeping you here? I'm asking for one night, Tom. One night only. You can stay, shower, and have some decent food and a warm bed. What's so wrong with a friend giving you that for one night?"

"It's what you'll want in exchange. Nothing comes for free, trust me. I learnt that the hard way."

"For fuck's sake, Tom, it's me! When have I ever asked for anything from you or anyone? I've always been there for my mates,

Take a Chance

you included. Why the fuck would that change now?"

Tom looked down to the ground, rubbing the back of his neck, face flushing. "I'm sorry, Seb. I know you're right. I'm just so used to things being different. It's how I've had to live for the past four years. It's not easy to trust."

"I know. I get it. The people you trusted the most let you down. I understand, Tom. I really do." Seb held out his hand to Tom again. "Come on. We can talk more when we get back to mine. Please."

Tom stared at Seb's hand. Should he take a chance on Seb? Should he give in this one time? Would he be weak to accept some help, even if it were for one night? He watched as Seb slowly lowered his hand, nod, and then turn to walk away.

"Okay, I'll come." Tom surprised himself when he spoke.

Seb turned back to Tom, eyes wide open. "Really?"

"Yeah." He followed Seb back to his car and got in the passenger side. Tom reached over and pulled the seatbelt on as Seb started the car and pulled away from the pavement. Within a couple of minutes, the warmth of the car seeped into his body and his eyes started to droop. His body felt heavy, the limbs difficult to move and the motions of the car seemed to help ease some of the tension he held. He blinked rapidly to try and stay alert. He couldn't fall asleep in anyone's car.

As they drove back to Seb's, he stared out of the window, watching the buildings as they flashed by, seeing the difference in the structures the further away from the city centre they travelled. The silence stretched in the car until it became unbearable, and Tom felt compelled to speak. "How long have you lived here?"

Seb glanced across at him. "Around two years now. When Nan died, I was left some money, and I used it as a deposit on a house, which I got cheap because it needs some work doing to it."

Tom snorted. "Must have been some inheritance."

"Yeah, I was really lucky, and as I said the house needs some work doing to it as in, it needs completely re-modernising. I'm still doing it now."

The car became silent again as Seb continued the drive to his. Turning into his driveway, Seb parked the car and switched the engine off. "Well, here we are," he advised as he got out.

Tom stared after Seb as he waited for him to follow, suddenly feeling uneasy. Maybe he had made a mistake coming here. He rubbed his sweaty palms on his jeans as his stomach tensed. Yeah, he knew Seb, but that was years ago and he could be a completely different man now. He'd stay for one drink then make up some excuse so he could leave. With his mind made up, he got out of the car and walked over to Seb trying to create some distance.

※ ※ ※

Seb noticed the difference in Tom immediately. Something had happened to him on the drive over here, and it was obviously nothing good by the stiff body posture he was now displaying. He appeared hunched up and couldn't look him in the eye.

Walking into his house, Seb turned to him, asking, "Do you want something to drink? I've got tea, coffee, beer, wine and maybe some Coke."

"Coffee, please." Tom rubbed his head. "Look, I can't stay long, so I'll have to go after the drink."

Ah, that was it. He'd decided to have a drink then leave. Seb didn't say anything as he walked into his kitchen but was aware of Tom following him.

Take a Chance

"Guess you weren't lying about the house needing some work doing to it."

Seb smiled as he looked at the kitchen. Yeah, it was definitely dated. It hadn't been touched in decades, probably the 1960s. Dark wood cabinets and white worktops, both tarnished or stained, with aqua blue tiles on almost all the walls. It was safe to say he didn't spend a lot of time in here or the dining room, which also needed updating. He usually came in from work and sat on the sofa to eat his dinner.

While the kettle was boiling, Seb thought about what he could do to help Tom. How could he keep Tom with him? What reason could he use to prevent him from leaving? To keep Tom safe. Short of offering him money--and really, how different was that to what he would be doing on the streets--he couldn't think of anything.

Seb decided to go with the direct approach and tell him what he wanted. "I don't want you to go back out there. Why not stay here tonight as you agreed. Have something to eat, drink, maybe a shower. Just relax."

Tom looked at him and slowly shook his head. He could see the argument starting to form in Tom's mind, so cut him off. "Please don't argue with me. I just...I don't know. I'm a solicitor, and I'm supposed to be good with words, but I don't know what to say that won't make you angry or chase you away." Seb took a couple of steps away, rubbing his hand through his short black hair. "It can't be good, can it? It can't feel good doing what you do. So just stay one night and not think about it. Spend the night with a friend."

"It can't feel good," Tom mimicked sarcastically, suddenly looking angry. "How d'ya think it fuckin' feels knowin' I'm just some hole to fuck, something someone's paid for? I knew it was a mistake coming here."

Tom stormed from the kitchen and walked to the front door ready to leave. Seb scrambled to catch up to him, grabbing his arm just as he got there. Tom spun around and snatched his arm out of Seb's hand, pushing him away and holding up a fist. Seb held up his hands in front of him trying to calm the situation.

"I'm sorry. I shouldn't have grabbed you like that. Please don't leave like this, Tom. Can't we just try and talk? I don't know what to say to you that won't make you pissed at me. I'm trying here."

Seb watched as Tom seemed to deflate suddenly in front of him, shoulders slumping, head dropping down towards his chest and closing his eyes as he leaned back against the door. He dropped his fist and opened his eyes to look at him, seeming far older than he was.

Seb smiled at him and held his hand out. "Come back through to the kitchen, and I'll finish the coffees." Seb turned and walked back towards the kitchen, praying that Tom followed him and didn't take this as an opportunity to leave. He got his answer when he heard Tom speak to him from behind.

"So, when ya plannin' on doin' the kitchen?"

Seb went with the change in conversation. Talking about the kitchen was probably the safest thing to discuss and would hopefully defuse the tension still present.

"Probably next year now, considering how close to Christmas we are. I've been lucky in that I've just been given a full-time contract at the solicitors I was doing my two year on-the-job training with. So I'll have more responsibility but also more money. Do you want milk and sugar?"

"Just milk please."

Seb finished making the drinks and handed one to him. "Come on. We'll sit in the living room."

Take a Chance

They walked into the living room, and Seb turned the radio on, making sure it was down low so it was in the background. Tom sat in the chair and glanced at Seb before he looked through the window outside. He looked ready to bolt at any second, his knee bouncing, and he kept turning the mug in his hands.

"Don't get mad at me, but can you tell me what actually happened that night? The night they kicked you out? Without shouting at me?" Seb smiled tentatively at Tom.

Tom sighed. "You want me to rake up all the dirt again?" Shrugging his shoulders, he said, "Sure, whatever. It's not gonna change anything now, is it?

"I don't mean it like that."

"It's alright Seb, I'll tell you. Liz found out she was pregnant, and because her parents knew mine, mine assumed it was me. I got in one night, and they confronted me with it. You can imagine my surprise at that, can't you? I mean, I'm gay, no chance I was the father, and that's what I told them. I'm thinking that supposedly getting some girl pregnant has got to be worse than having a gay son, right? Well, I got that wrong." Tom sipped his coffee before continuing. "They looked stunned at first, then horrified, and I knew then that I was wrong. Being gay was far worse. Their faces became, like, twisted, you know. It's hard to describe, but I remember thinking that the shit was gonna hit the fan.

"Next thing, my dad has got hold of my arm, and he's dragging me out of the lounge towards the front door. I'm screaming at him to let me go, but he didn't. He just threw me out the front door, calling me twisted and perverted and to never come back, that I was no son of theirs. It seemed they preferred an unplanned teenage pregnancy to a gay son. I tried to let myself back in, to talk to them, but they'd locked the door. So I walked over to your parents' house. Thought maybe they'd help. I knocked on the front door, and your mum answered. She just looked at me and then spat at me. Told me to fuck off, that they didn't want my kind around, corrupting their son. And Josh? He was watching from the window, and then he closed the curtains. In the time it had taken for me to walk over, my parents had spoken to yours and had told them everything." Tom stopped talking at that point and stared at the mug in his hands.

Seb winced. "I'm so sorry. They should never have done that to you."

"Doesn't matter now, does it? Anyway, I walked around a bit, lost, and I didn't know what to do. It was raining, and I didn't have much money on me and only the clothes on my back. I figured I'd give them a day to calm down and get used to the idea, and then I would go back. So I found a shed and spent the night in there, but I was too scared to sleep. Next morning, I went back and tried to get in, but again I couldn't. So I went around the back and tried again, but my key wouldn't work. That was when I realised they'd had the locks changed. I hadn't even been gone a day, and they'd changed the locks." Tom snorted, anger blazing in his blue eyes as he stared at Seb.

Seb looked at him, mouth dropping open. It just got worse and worse, didn't it? How could anyone's parents do that to their child because of their sexuality? How could they treat their son so callously? He sat there at a loss as to what to say and watched Tom drink his coffee, staring out the window, seemingly lost in his memories.

"Why don't you stay tonight? Have a shower, some food or whatever."

"I can't," Tom whispered.

"Is it because of the money?" Tom looked at him, and Seb could see how tired he was. Why can't he just have this one night to relax?

"Fuck, Tom, where are you living?"

"Honestly?"

Take a Chance

Seb nodded.

"An abandoned house."

"Then stay here tonight."

"And what about tomorrow, Seb? Would you just let me walk out of here? Could you?"

Seb looked away from Tom, unable to answer him because he wasn't sure what the answer would be, but he figured it would probably be no.

"I thought so. I think it's best I leave, don't you?" Tom stood up as he spoke, and Seb followed him as he walked to the front door.

"What can I say to make you stay? Do I offer you money? Do I ask you to stay the weekend or ask you to move in? Because I can't let you leave, knowing what you do and where you live. You're my friend, someone I've known for years. I can't let you walk away. I just can't."

"This isn't your problem to fix, Seb."

"I know, but just give me tonight. Please. Don't you want just one night away from it all?" Seb would beg if he had to.

He could see how torn Tom was over it by the way he refused to meet his stare. It was obvious that he wanted to stay but for some reason, he wouldn't. He knew he had trust issues. He'd admitted it himself. Tom suddenly looked up at him and sighed as he nodded his head. The tension in Seb's body left, and he sighed as he nodded back at him. He was starting to relax knowing he was going to stay.

"I'll show you to the guest room. I've not done anything with it, but it does have a double bed in it, and it's warm."

Seb walked up the stairs, making sure Tom followed him and opened the door to the guest room. Ugly woodchip wallpaper decorated the walls with a dark brown carpet on the floor. Black curtains hung over the window.

"I know it's not much, but it's yours for the night." He pointed to the bathroom and explained, "Over here is the bathroom, with spare towels, and there's a new toothbrush under the sink." Seb rubbed the back of his neck as he looked at the wallpaper, surprisingly nervous. "I'll just head downstairs now and leave you to it. Oh, I'll leave some spare clothes outside. Bring down yours and I'll wash them."

"Thanks," Tom murmured quietly.

Seb smiled. "You're welcome."

As he walked down the stairs, he heard the bathroom door open and then close and not long after, the shower started. He felt better than he had done since he'd first seen Tom on that street. Now he just had to come up with an idea to stop him from going back out there.

Take a Chance

Chapter Eight

Tom stood under the hot water and closed his eyes as he lifted his head to let the water spray over his face. When was the last time he'd enjoyed a hot shower? Too long. He couldn't remember the last time. Finding the toiletries, Tom spent a long time cleaning himself, not knowing when the next time would be. His skin reddened as he scrubbed it while the water warmed him. He sighed, closing his eyes, his shoulders dropping. He rotated his head under the spray, releasing the tension from his aching muscles.

After a few more minutes, he switched the shower off and stepped out, reaching for a towel and drying himself. He opened the bathroom door and looked down, finding the clothes Seb said he would leave for him. They were close to the same size, with Seb maybe an inch or two on Tom, so the clothes weren't too big on him. He lifted them to his nose and inhaled, smelling the fabric conditioner Seb had used.

Getting dressed, he searched in the cabinet under the sink, finding the new toothbrush, and brushed his teeth. He brushed them again and ran his tongue over them. When he was sure they felt clean, he put the toothbrush on the side. Feeling cleaner than he had done in a long time, he picked up his dirty clothes and went downstairs looking for Seb.

In the kitchen, Tom found Seb cooking. He stood and watched for a few seconds, admiring the way he moved around the kitchen. Seb smiled at him when he saw him and pointed to a door on the other side of the kitchen. "The washing machine is in there. Just throw them in. I made you some food. Want to eat in front of the TV?"

Tom nodded and quickly put his clothes in the machine before picking up his plate, smiling. Macaroni cheese. One of his favourites.

Going into the lounge, Tom sat on the chair. Looking at the TV, he turned to Seb. "Is that *The Terminator*?"

"Yeah, I love this film." Seb sat on the sofa and started to eat his food.

"I remember. You always had it on."

"You don't mind, do you?"

"No, I've not seen anything in years."

Seb didn't answer, and Tom turned to look at him, noticing the way Seb was watching him and the look on his face. A look of pity and maybe guilt, which he chose to ignore. He started to eat his food and moaned at the taste. Freshly cooked food that was free of grease or slime. Tasted fantastic. Another thing he missed. When he finished eating, he took his plate out and came back in to continue watching the film.

Next thing he knew, he was being shaken gently awake. "Hey, wanna go to bed?"

Tom looked up at him, blinking his eyes rapidly, scratching his cheek. He glanced around the room before remembering where he was. "Yeah, thanks. How long was I asleep for?"

"About an hour or so. I'm heading up now so..."

Tom watched as Seb walked towards the stairs and nodded his head, even though Seb couldn't see him, and stood up to follow him upstairs.

"Night, Tom." Seb smiled at him before closing his bedroom door.

Tom walked into his room and also closed the door. Walking over to the bed, he stripped off and climbed under the covers. He lay there enjoying the softness of the mattress and covers thick enough to keep him warm, running his hands over them repeatedly. Within a few minutes, he'd drifted back off to sleep again.

※ ※ ※

Tom woke to find himself in a strange room and sat up quickly as his heart pounded rapidly in his chest. He scanned the room before he remembered where he was. He lay back down as he blew out his breath and closed his eyes, listening to the sounds of the house, realising that Seb was already up. He looked out the window to see that it was light outside. He squinted his eyes as he turned his head away from the sun and decided it was time to get up.

He spotted his clothes on a chair and paused as he realised that Seb had been in the room while he had slept and had left them for him. He frowned, not quite sure how he felt about Seb being in the room while he'd been asleep, but he'd washed and dried his clothes for him. Walking over, he picked them up and smelled them, rubbing them against his face, relishing the fresh, clean scent they held. No matter how many times he had washed his clothes, they never held that fresh, clean smell. Putting them back down on the chair, he left the bedroom and went downstairs.

He could smell something delicious cooking, and his stomach rumbled in agreement. When he walked into the kitchen, he found Seb piling bacon onto a plate. He turned and smiled at him before asking, "Did you sleep well?"

Tom nodded. "Yeah, I did. Thanks for washing my stuff," he said as he rubbed the back of his neck and glanced at the floor.

"No problem. It seems like you needed the sleep. You didn't stir at all when I brought your clothes in. I figured you could do with a lie in. I was going to come up anyway as I've made bacon sandwiches for lunch."

"Lunch? Is it that late?" he asked as he dropped his hand. He hadn't realised he had slept in so late.

Seb handed him a plate and a cup of coffee while smiling. "Don't worry about it. Come on."

Tom followed Seb through to the lounge and sat down in the same chair from the night before. He bit his lip, peeking at Seb. What was going to happen now? What would Seb say now it was morning? What would he want? No one had been nice to him in such a long time without wanting something in return. He sat quietly and started eating his food, glancing at Seb, who wasn't paying him any attention, his eyes glued to the TV. As he looked around the room, he knew he didn't belong here. His stomach tightened, and he swallowed his mouth dry. This wasn't a place for someone like him. He didn't deserve to be here.

After he had finished eating, he stood up. "Thanks, Seb, for everything, but I think it's time that I left."

"What? Why?" Seb looked up at him wide-eyed.

Take a Chance

"I need to get back, and I just can't stay. Thanks for last night." He walked into the kitchen and put his plate and cup in the sink. He turned to find Seb behind him frowning, confusion showing on his face.

"You can stay, you know. You don't have to leave."

Tom leaned back onto the counter, facing Seb. "I don't want to argue with you, alright? I don't, but this--" he waved his hand in the air-- "this is your home and I don't belong here. I have to go."

Tom brushed past him as he walked out of the kitchen and then jogged upstairs so he could change his clothes. Seb followed him and walked into the guest room behind him.

"You don't have to go," Seb told him.

"And I can't stay either."

"Why? What's stopping you? You can stay as long as you want." The frustration was evident in his voice as he spoke to Tom and paced the floor.

"Why? Why are you doing this? Is it some guilt trip because your fuckin' parents and Josh turned their backs on me? This isn't on you. This isn't your fault." He turned away as he started to undress aware that Seb hadn't left the room and was stood there watching him. "You gonna fuckin' watch me get changed?"

Seb spun around. "Don't leave."

Tom finished changing and walked up to Seb, handing him the clothes he had worn. "I have to go," he mumbled as he walked past him and jogged downstairs.

Seb followed him to the front door. "Are you going out tonight?" He glared at Tom.

Tom hesitated as he was walking out and then turned to face him. "What do you think?"

"Then I'll pay for you, for tonight."

"What the fuck? No!" The thought of Seb paying him....

"You won't stay here, and you need the money, so why the fuck not? What are you saying, Tom? Strangers can pay to fuck you, but I can't pay for you to stay? If I have to pay for the night, I will."

Tom stared at Seb for a minute, taking in the clenched jaw and fists, before turning and walking away.

"If you change your mind, you know where I am," Seb shouted before slamming the door behind him causing Tom to jump.

※ ※ ※

Seb stood by the window and watched Tom walk away, shoulders slumped over and with his head hanging low, and wondered if he had made the right choice in letting him go. He knew if he'd continued to try to convince him to stay, they would have ended up arguing, and that would have pushed Tom further away. He groaned when he thought about what he'd said. He shouldn't have offered to pay for him, but the words just popped out of his mouth before he had even thought about them. He had to trust that Tom would work his way through whatever it was that was stopping him accepting his help. Yes, he understood the reasons why he struggled to trust him, but there seemed to be something else going on inside his head. He couldn't help him if he wasn't going to let him in. He'd known him for years, but now it seemed like a complete stranger had taken his place. Well, maybe that was true. Tom had probably seen and done a lot of things Seb didn't know about, and that had to change you as a person. He sighed as he sat on the sofa and dropped his head in his hands.

What could he do? What could he say to help Tom see that the life he was living wasn't the one he deserved? That there was better out there for him if he only took a chance and reached for it. Did Tom want to escape his life? Or did he think he deserved it? No, he couldn't think he deserved it. No one should be abandoned by their parents because they were gay. No one should be turned away by their friends because of their sexuality.

He leaned back on the sofa and closed his eyes as he thought about the first time he noticed Tom. The first time he saw him as something other than his brother's friend. That had scared the shit out of him. He'd always had girlfriends before and suddenly, one summer, he saw him cleaning his dad's car with Josh, and he had looked gorgeous. He'd made a point to come home as often as he could so that he spent time with him. But he had never mentioned anything to him. He hadn't known Tom was gay, and at the time, he hadn't been so sure about himself either. Uni had changed that for him, and his friendship with Fin.

Now Seb wondered how he could save Tom from this life, and he couldn't come up with a single answer. How do you help someone who doesn't want your help, even if they need it?

※ ※ ※

Tom dressed for work that night even though he didn't want to, and the weather had turned nasty. He had no money and desperately needed some. He had to force himself to get up and dressed, telling himself that there was no alternative, even though that was a lie.

He went to his usual spot, trying not to throw up, and it wasn't long before a car slowed down and stopped next to him. Plastering a smile on his face, he walked over as the window was wound down. The stench from inside the car hit him, and he took a step back, recoiling from the odour. He'd been with guys before with rank body odour, but this was way beyond that. Standing, staring at the car, Tom began to wonder why he hadn't taken Seb up on his offer. Sleeping in his spare room was infinitely better than this shit. He prayed the guy didn't want a blow job. "Hi, what do you want?"

The bloke looked up at him, and Tom could see the greasy hair and was that food in his beard? "Everything." Aaannnnndddd his day went from bad to worse.

Backing away, swallowing against the bile that was forcing its way up his throat, he smiled as he told him, "Not tonight. Sorry."

"Not tonight? I'm pretty sure I've fucked you before, and you seemed eager then. I'll pay double."

"Look, I'm not interested."

Tom turned and walked away, trying to get away from the guy as quickly as possible. Suddenly, he was slammed face first into a wall, the bricks scratching across his face. He tried to turn, but was punched in the ribs, forcing his breath to explode out of him as pain radiated across his abdomen. He tried to force air into his lungs, but winced as his ribs protested. He could feel a hand groping around his crotch and the button of his jeans being undone. He struggled to push himself away from the wall and threw an elbow back hoping to catch the guy, but he was slammed back into the wall, his head banging painfully against it. He gritted his teeth against the pain and tried to yell.

"Stay the fuck still. This won't take long."

"Get off me," he screamed. Tom was suddenly spun around and punched in the face. Pain exploded up around his eye and along his cheek, causing him to close his eyes as he tried to lift his hands up to defend himself. Another punch in the stomach had him doubling over, his breath exploding out of him again. He was slammed face first into the wall again, his jeans being pushed down below his arse.

Take a Chance

Panicking, he shouted as loud as he could, hoping to draw attention to what was happening as he bucked and pushed back against the man who was trying to force his cock into him. Luck was with him as he heard someone yelling from further up the street and the sound of running feet reached him. Suddenly released, he slumped down to the ground, hearing the car door slam and the engine revving before pulling away. He pulled his jeans up and got back up slowly using the wall to help him. His face and ribs pulsed in pain, and he leaned against the wall catching his breath.

"Hey, you alright?"

He opened his eyes to see two men stood in front of him. He smiled weakly and nodded his head. "Yeah, I am." Pushing away from the wall, he started to walk along the street.

"Don't you need to go to the hospital?"

"No, no thanks. I'd rather just forget about it." He continued walking, going faster and faster until he was running flat out. That was when he felt the first drops of rain hit his face.

※ ※ ※

Seb was getting ready for bed when he heard the doorbell ring. Looking at the clock, he was surprised that anyone would be calling this late at night. Grabbing a robe, he ran downstairs and opened the door. He paused, mouth falling open at seeing Tom stood there, wet through and bleeding. He quickly forgot his anger at Tom as he stared at him.

"Jesus, what the fuck happened to you?" Seb managed to gasp out.

"Can I come in?" Tom asked as he squinted his eyes against the rain dripping into them from his soaked hair.

"What? Of course, you can. Go straight upstairs to the bathroom. We need to get you out of those wet clothes and see to your face. What happened, Tom?"

Tom grimaced and walked past him to go upstairs, not bothering to answer. Seb followed and watched him start stripping. He turned away, suddenly conscious of all that naked flesh in front of him. God, how perverted was he to be getting a hard on when Tom was wet and bleeding, the victim of an assault. Seb groaned and mentally slapped himself.

Seb went to his room and grabbed some clean clothes before going back to the bathroom. He looked at Tom again, and it hit him how skinny he truly was. His ribs and collar bones stood out, and his limbs seemed too thin.

"Here, let me look at your face."

Tom turned to face him, wearing nothing but a towel around his hips. Seb could feel himself start to blush and grabbed the first aid box. He glanced at him and realised that Tom was completely unaware of the state he was in. There was blood dripping from his eye, and it looked like it was starting to swell shut. He had a swollen cheek and Seb could see the beginning of a bruise forming from around his eye and onto his cheek. He also had scratches on both sides of his face but from what, Seb wasn't sure. He had a red contusion on his ribs that looked painful. Tom's long hair was dripping rainwater, and even though he'd been wearing clothes, his skin was wet, with droplets of water running down. With a sigh, he stepped close and gently held his chin, looking at his eye.

"Doesn't seem like it'll need stitches, but I want to put a couple of strips on it, just to keep it closed while it heals. Take a shower and I'll do it when you get downstairs. Here," he handed him the clothes, "put these on."

Picking up the first aid box, he shut the door and walked

Take a Chance

downstairs. He groaned to himself when he was out of earshot. How could he have been turned on when Tom looked like shit? Sure, he was virtually naked, but he should have better control than that. What would Tom have thought if he'd noticed?

He put the kettle on and grabbed the things he'd need to make coffee, and then put some leftover stew in the microwave to heat up. He stood, listening to the shower running in the bathroom, and wondered how he could convince Tom to stop what he was doing. It was obvious something had happened and with the news about the attacks, he was worried that something far worse would occur.

He looked up at the ceiling when he heard the shower shut off and finished making the drinks, checking the food to make sure it was hot. He turned and smiled at Tom as he walked into the kitchen. He reached out and took his wet clothes before nodding to the food.

"Have some stew, it's only heated up leftovers, and there's coffee as well."

He went into the utility room and put Tom's clothes in the washing machine, starting a wash cycle. When he returned, he found Tom had taken his food and had sat on the sofa in the living room. Tom didn't look at him when Seb sat down next to him.

"What happened?"

Tom sighed and put his spoon down as he avoided looking at him and Seb watched as he rubbed his eyes then winced as he touched the cut. Again, Seb couldn't help but notice that he seemed so much older than his years. Older and tired, like he had the weight of the world on his shoulders.

"I couldn't do it. The guy fuckin' stank and I walked away. He didn't want to take no for an answer, so we got into a fight."

"And that's it? What would have happened if you hadn't gotten away?"

Tom narrowed his eyes at him. "What do you think?"

Not wanting to cause an argument, he let the comment go. He picked up the first aid box and twisted to face Tom. "Let me see to your eye."

He removed the strips out of the first-aid kit and cut them into the lengths that he needed, and then applied them carefully to the cut. Tom's blue eyes watched him the entire time, but he didn't say a word. Seb could feel the tension in the air between them.

"It sounds like you were lucky this time. What about next time, Tom? Are you still going to keep doing this and risking yourself?"

"I don't know," Tom whispered. "What choice do I have?"

Seb looked up at him from where he was kneeling on the floor. "Think about it, for me. Finish your food and relax for a while, alright?"

Tom nodded then suddenly seemed to notice what he was wearing. "Were you goin' to bed?"

"Yeah, but I can stay up with you if you want the company. We can watch another film together. What do you say? You are staying the night, aren't you?"

"D'ya mind? Don't think I can go out again tonight." Tom looked so lost and defeated, head dropping onto his chest, and Seb's heart ached for him.

"Remember, I didn't want you to leave in the first place? Watch a film. We can talk more in the morning."

"I'd rather just go to bed."

Seb nodded. "Yeah okay. You go up. I need to lock up again."

Seb took Tom's dishes and washed them before he locked the front door and walked upstairs. The light in Tom's room was off, so he

Take a Chance

assumed he was sleeping. Closing the door to his room, he undressed and slipped under the cool covers. He laid thinking about Tom and what had been an attempted rape. Tom didn't have to say the words, but you'd have to be an idiot not to know that's what had happened. At least, he had come to him for help. That was something, wasn't it?

Chapter Nine

Tom woke, but this time he knew where he was. He started to stretch, then suddenly groaned, squeezing his eyes shut and groaning again as he breathed in deeply through his mouth. He waited for the pain to lessen. Fuck, that hurt!

Opening his eyes, Tom stared at the ceiling, wondering what the fuck he was going to do. He'd come straight here last night, hadn't even thought about going anywhere else. Sighing, he rolled over carefully, wincing as he did, and looked at the chair. His clothes weren't there, and then he remembered why. They were probably still in the washer downstairs.

Throwing back the covers, Tom whimpered, holding his breath as he attempted to stand on wobbly legs. He took several deep breaths before he felt he could move and staggered to the bathroom to freshen up.

Take a Chance

Looking in the mirror, he groaned again when he saw the state of his face. The bruising hadn't looked too bad last night, but while he slept, it had time to settle. His face now looked a mess with his eye and cheek covered in black and blue bruising. His eye was also partly swollen shut. The bruising only seemed to highlight the white colour of the strips Seb had put on his eyebrow last night. He lifted up the shirt he was wearing and gingerly touched his side, sucking in a breath as he touched the tender skin. It didn't look too bad though, and the bruising was only minimal.

Seeing the toothbrush he'd used still on the sink brought a smile to Tom's face. Seb had kept it for him. He suddenly frowned. Why had he kept it? How had he known he would come back? Why did it matter? Shrugging, he brushed his teeth and carefully walked downstairs, wincing every time he felt his body protest. His clothes were in the washer but were dry, so he took them out and quickly changed before he put in Seb's. Looking around the kitchen, he saw Seb's wallet. He hadn't worked Friday or Saturday night and was in desperate need of money, but could he do what he was thinking of doing? Robbing a stranger was one thing; robbing someone he knew was another matter.

Tom walked away grabbing his hair as he did, torn between his need and doing the right thing by Seb. If he did this, would Seb forgive him? Did he care? He snorted. Of course he cared. Seb was the first person from his old life who saw him and didn't flinch away when confronted with the truth. Fuck, being a rent boy hadn't bothered him, and he hadn't been the least bit concerned about the fact that he was gay.

Making his decision, he grabbed Seb's wallet and opened it, quickly looking through the compartments. He grabbed the notes and shoved them in his front pocket, throwing the wallet back on the counter. As he was leaving the kitchen, he saw a pad and pen, and he bit his lip as he shuffled his feet.

Eventually, he wrote 'I'm sorry' before he left the house. Glancing at the clock, he saw that was just after ten. It was Sunday. The shops would be opening soon, so he could grab a bite to eat and then do a quick shop. He now had close to two hundred quid, and that would easily last a couple of weeks if not longer if he was careful.

It took him almost thirty minutes to walk into the city centre, and Tom was hot and sweaty, even though it wasn't warm. By the time he reached the centre, shops were beginning to open. He stopped in a cafe and ordered a full English breakfast, devouring it quickly, then did some shopping at the local supermarket. He was conscious of the stares he was receiving from people as he walked around, people looking him up and down or just staring at his bruised face. He tried to shield his face as best he could and avoided looking at anyone directly, but he was still aware of them. Once he finished shopping, he quickly walked home, ready to escape the looks.

The house was quiet when Tom walked in, so he put the food in the kitchen and sat down on the floor in the living room, rubbing his arms and shoulders to ease the ache he felt in them from carrying the heavy bags. Now he had stopped moving, he started to think about what he'd done to Seb. He bit his lip and slumped over as he closed his eyes. His stomach rolled, and Tom swallowed, sure he was going to be sick. He took several deep breaths until it settled, then leaned back.

Seb was going to be pissed off. Had he pushed Seb too far by stealing from him? Would Seb ever forgive him? Seb had been nice to him, caring for his injuries, feeding him and letting him sleep over, and he'd repaid him by stealing from him. The more he thought about what he had done, the worse he felt. But it was too late to change it now. Seb would have grown tired of him anyway and it wasn't like he had anything to offer him. He was only good at one, no, maybe two things. Fucks and blow jobs and Seb wasn't gay, so that was a no. He shook his head. It wasn't like him to feel sorry for himself. He had taken what life had dealt him and done the best he could. Wallowing in self-pity would get him nowhere.

Tom looked up when he heard noises from above and sighed. He couldn't leave these guys, not with everything that was going on. He closed his eyes and opened them when Ben walked into the room.

"Tom, where were you last night?" Ben stopped, and his jaw dropped open when he caught sight of Tom's face. "What the fuck happened to you?"

"I said no, and the punter wasn't happy."

"Did he...did he do..." Ben took a deep breath in before continuing. "Did he do anything else to you?"

"No. I was able to get away." There was no need to go into details about what had happened.

"So, where did you go?"

Tom sighed. "I was at an old friend's house."

Ben raised his eyebrows at him. "An old friend's house. Did he see to your eye?"

Tom nodded. "Yeah. He was great actually. Wasn't happy about what happened to me."

"And you left to come back here? What the fuck are you doing? You could be in a nice warm house, away from all this shit, or doesn't he know about what you do?" Ben frowned at Tom.

"He knows."

"So what's the problem? Why aren't you there?"

Tom shrugged. "None, I guess. He wanted me to stay."

"So, again why did you leave? If he can give you a way out, then why haven't you taken it?" Ben frowned.

"It's not that simple." Tom sighed as he rubbed his head with his hand. He didn't want to tell Ben he had robbed Seb.

"Why not? We're all here because there was nothing else for us, but you might just have a chance to escape this, to make something better of your life. If I were you, I'd take it."

Tom shook his head. "What about you guys? Who would be there for you?"

"Don't think about us. We'll manage somehow. Look, if any one of us had the chance that you might have, we'd take it."

"Take what?" Adam muttered as he staggered into the room, more asleep than awake, rubbing his eyes.

Ben scowled at Adam. "What the fuck do you think you were doing last night goin' off on your own like that? Didn't you learn anything from the beating you got last time?" Ben crossed his arms over his chest and stared at Adam.

"It's nothing." Adam glared at Ben.

"Nothing!" Ben spat at him. Turning to Tom, he said, "One minute he's stood there and the next he's gone." Ben faced Adam. "You're gonna end up beaten to a pulp and left for dead somewhere. You know whoever is doing this shit is getting more dangerous."

Tom stood and stared at Adam, his mouth falling open as he gasped. "Fuck, man. Why would you risk yourself like that? Look at the state of me! I didn't have back up and almost paid for it."

"We're all alone at some fuckin' point, aren't we? We wouldn't get the fuckin' job done." Adam glared at them.

"I know that, but we stick together for details of the car or the man. If one of us goes missing, at least we have details for the cops," Ben argued.

"What? Like they give a shit about people like us. They probably think those blokes are doing them a fuckin' favour, getting rid of a couple of fags like us." Adam sneered. "I'm sick of this bullshit. If I wanna go out and work on my own, then I fuckin' will." He stormed out of the room, and Tom could hear him banging the board on the kitchen door behind him as he left the house.

Tom turned to Ben, who was staring at the door, eyes tight as he glared at the door Adam had just stormed through. "I can't believe he did it again."

"You and me both. He's gonna end up dead the way he's goin'. He doesn't give a shit about his safety, just the money. He doesn't need to do anything either because he made a couple of hundred over the weekend, but I don't think that'll stop him. I just don't know what's fuckin' wrong with him." Ben rubbed his hands through his hair and grunted. "I don't know what to say to him either. Nothing seems to get through."

"Maybe it's just his way of dealing with what happened. It's only been a week since the attack. If it carries on, then we should try talking to him, see what's goin' on."

Ben looked at the floor, as he pulled his bottom lip. Nodding, he sighed and walked out of the room, leaving Tom standing there watching him go. He sat and took the money out of his pocket, counting how much he had left. He put it on the floor in front of him and sat staring at it. He had sunk to a new low, stealing it. Seb had been nothing but kind and generous to him, offering him a place to stay, and this was how he'd repaid him. He moved the coins around with his fingers as he continued to think about what he had done. Would Seb forgive him? More importantly, could he forgive himself?

※ ※ ※

Seb spent most of the week alternating between two emotions:

disappointed and furious. He'd been trying to help Tom, opening his home to him, giving him food, a warm and dry place to sleep. Seb hadn't expected Tom to fall at his feet in gratitude, but he didn't expect Tom to steal from him either. Yeah, he definitely became angry thinking about that.

However, when Seb calmed down, which did take some time, he could understand why he had done it. Maybe he was too proud to ask for help, or he had been doing this for too long and it was all he knew, or maybe he was just too afraid to trust anyone again. Seb was lucky. He had his parents and a family home he'd been able to grow up in. He'd had the opportunity to go to Uni and get the job he had wanted. This was only because he hadn't told his parents the truth about his sexuality.

Tom hadn't had any of those things. His parents had taken those choices away from him and left him to fend for himself at the age of fifteen.

Friday was the worst day, as all he could think about was whether Tom would be working that night and hoping that he wasn't. Surely two hundred quid would last him longer than a few days. He knew he lived in a house with no gas or electricity, so he wouldn't have bills to pay, just food and drink. Or was he buying drugs? He didn't seem like he was doing drugs, and he hadn't seen any obvious physical marks on his body. He didn't have that look to him, but what did he know? Tom looked like he had his head screwed on, even given the circumstances.

Sighing, Seb closed down his computer. He couldn't stay in another Friday night on the off chance Tom would turn up, and he didn't think he would. It would seem he'd gotten what he'd wanted. He stood up and grabbed his bag and coat before leaving his desk.

He hadn't gotten very far before he heard his name called.

"Seb, can you come in here for a minute." Looking up, he saw Geoff stood by his open office door and walked over to him.

"Close the door and take a seat."

Seb frowned, but did as he was asked and waited for Geoff to speak to him. He wasn't aware of doing anything wrong, so couldn't figure out why he'd been called in.

As he waited for Geoff to speak, Seb tried to swallow, his mouth suddenly dry. He wiped his clammy hands on his pants, breathing deeply to keep calm.

"I just wanted to catch up and see how you're doing. I've noticed you seem a little distracted, and I wanted to make sure we hadn't put too much on you too soon."

Seb's mouth opened as he stared at Geoff. First, he hadn't thought his performance had been that affected by what was going on outside of work, and secondly, he didn't think anyone would have noticed. "No, no everything's fine."

"So if it's not work, what is it?" Geoff stared at him intently as he leaned on his desk, waiting for him to answer.

"It's nothing." Seb smiled, hoping to reassure Geoff that everything was alright. He didn't want to discuss this with anyone in work. He didn't even know if he could find the words to describe it. How did you tell someone that a person you knew had sex for money? That they were a prostitute?

"Well, I'm here if you want to talk about it." He smiled at him. "Get going now. It's Friday, and you've probably got plans, right?"

Nodding, Seb stood up. "Yeah, out with some mates. I'll see you Monday."

Seb left the office and walked over to where he had parked his car. He hadn't planned on going to the gym, so drove straight home, but as it was rush hour, it took almost an hour before he pulled into his drive. As he did, he noticed someone sat on the step outside his house. The person looked up when he heard the car, and Seb found himself staring at Tom.

Seb breathed in deeply when he saw him sat there. What the fuck! How dare he come back after what he'd done? Seb sat gripping the steering wheel, his knuckles turning white with how tight he was holding it. He could feel the tension in his jaw and shoulders and willed himself to calm down, but it was difficult. He glared at Tom through the windscreen and ground his teeth together, nostrils flaring.

Closing his eyes, he tried to regain control. There had to be a reason he would come back here after he had stolen from him. Seb took another deep breath and slowly relaxed his grip on the steering wheel, feeling the tightness in his knuckles ease. Whatever reasons he had, he didn't want to hear them.

Grabbing his things, Seb got out of the car and slowly walked over to Tom, who by now had stood up and was looking everywhere but at him. "What do you want?"

Tom looked at him before quickly glancing away. "I came to apologise."

"Really? You've got my money then?" Tom looked away again. "Yeah, didn't think so. Goodbye, Tom." He went to open the door when he heard Tom speak.

"Please, Seb. I know I fucked up, and I'm sorry, really sorry. Just give me a chance."

Seb looked at him, seeing the sincerity in the expression on his face. He turned back to the door and opened it. "Come in," he muttered. Sighing, he walked in, leaving the door open behind him, and went into the kitchen dropping his bags on the floor. He filled the kettle and turned to face Tom again. He was still angry and a part of him, a huge part of him, wanted to punch him. But instead, he asked him, "Have you eaten?"

"No." Tom shook his head as he fidgeted. He couldn't seem to settle himself. He had his hands in his pockets, and then he had them in front of his stomach, and then he was running them through his shaggy blond hair. Seb could see how nervous he was, and he wasn't too proud to admit it, but a small part of him enjoyed it.

"Fancy a curry? I'll phone up and get it delivered. Oh, and Tom, you're paying." Seb went to leave the kitchen but turned and looked back at him. "I'm going upstairs to change. I expect you to be here when I come back down." Seb told Tom in a firm voice, leaving no doubt in Tom's mind that he meant what he said.

He left Tom standing there with eyes open wide and his mouth hanging open as he went upstairs to his room. He sat on his bed and dropped his head in his hands. What was he doing? Was he really going to help him again after everything? Yeah, of course he was because Tom had come to him and had waited for him to arrive home so that he could apologise. They were going to talk when he went downstairs whether Tom liked it or not. He wanted to know more about what was going on in Tom's life. They hadn't discussed any of that in great detail. They'd talked about why he was on the streets and his parent's involvement, but other than that, all he knew was that he lived in an abandoned house and sold himself. Yes, they were important facts about him, but there was more to his life than that. He didn't appear to take drugs or drink, so what was he doing to keep himself going? Everyone heard about how prostitution was rife with drug addicts and alcoholics, but Tom seemed to be pretty clued up, so how was he doing it?

Stripping off, he had a shower and dressed quickly. As he was leaving his bedroom, he heard the doorbell go and knew the food had arrived. Good timing.

Seb jogged down the stairs and walked into the kitchen just as Tom brought in the bag of food. He already had plates and cutlery out.

Tom turned to Seb as he put the bag down on the counter and started unloading the boxes. "Is it alright that I got things out?" he asked shyly.

"Yep, less for me to do. I'm starving." Seb started to heap food on his plate before turning to Tom and asking, "Beer?" Tom nodded, so he grabbed two bottles from the fridge, and with his plate, went into the lounge and sat. Tom followed, and for a few minutes, neither of them talked while they ate their food.

"So, I've decided we're going to talk, and you're going to give me answers, alright? I think it's the least I deserve, all things considered." He saw Tom swallow before he took a deep breath and nodded.

"You said you live in an abandoned house. Alone? With others?"

"I live with four others."

"Younger, older?"

"One my age and the other three are younger, and yeah, they do the same thing."

"How did you meet?"

Tom shrugged. "Just while working. I saw Matt and Luke together, and they seemed so young but they're seventeen, older than I was. They hadn't been doing it long, and I didn't want them to make the same mistakes I had. Don't get me wrong. I tried to talk them out of it. But they said they couldn't go back home for some reason, and I didn't want to push them for an answer." He paused, then continued, "Er, Ben...I've known for about a year on and off and then there's Adam. I think he's my age. I'm most worried about him."

"Why? Is he doing drugs or something?"

"Nah, I don't think so." Tom shook his head. "He was beaten up a couple of weeks ago and almost kidnapped. People look out for one another on the street, and few live together the way we do, but it works

Take a Chance

for us. None of us wants to be doing this shit. We try to go out in pairs so one can keep an eye on things when the other is busy. You know the make and model of the car and the registration if possible. It's safer that way, but one night Adam didn't fuckin' do that, and he was lucky he only got a beating. Since then, it seems like he's become reckless, according to Ben."

"I've heard about the violence. It seems to be getting worse."

"Yeah, that's why we try to go in pairs. Don't want to get fucked up."

Seb looked away thinking about what he'd heard. He didn't want Tom out on the streets. He looked back at him. "Why did you do it? Why did you take the money?" he asked before he thought better of it.

Tom looked down and rubbed his hands together. Seb watched as he bit his lip and his cheeks flushed pink. "That's why I came here. I couldn't live with it. It's one thing to rob a stranger, but another to rob someone I know." He reached into his back pocket and pulled out a few notes. "I don't have much left, but here, you can have it back."

Seb gaped at him. "Have you any idea how insulting that is?"

Tom looked stunned, his blue eyes wide, and stuttered, "I'm sorry...I just thought..."

"Keep it. Just tell me you used it for something you needed."

He nodded. "Yeah, I bought food. None of us will have to go out if we don't want to for a few days now."

"Well, at least something good came from it."

Tom stood. "I need to go. Thanks for everything."

Seb growled. "Not this again. You know you can stay. Hell, stay the weekend. We can talk and try to figure something out." He stood up and grabbed the plates, stomping into the kitchen, pissed off at Tom for wanting to leave again. Why couldn't he just accept his help? He practically threw the plates into the sink and leaned against it. Damn, Tom. Why was he always pushing him away?

He pushed away from the counter and turned, bumping into Tom, not realising he had followed him. He stared into Tom's blue eyes and watched as the pupils dilated. Tom licked his lips, and Seb copied the action. His nostrils flared as he caught Tom's scent and he hardened in his jeans. He hadn't been this close to him other than when he'd been fixing his cut eye, and he suddenly had the overwhelming urge to kiss him. Seb looked down at Tom's lips and watched as they parted.

He reached a hand up and gently touched Tom's cheek, feeling the stubble on his jaw. Leaning forward, he paused, waiting for Tom to push him away or to speak and when he didn't, he touched his lips to Tom's and felt him inhale sharply. Nothing happened for a second, and then Tom hesitantly kissed him back, just a meeting of lips, a series of small kisses before they both pulled away, looking at each other.

He stepped back and looked at Tom, noting the stunned expression on his face, and he quickly apologised. "I'm sorry, I shouldn't have done that." He cleared his throat. "I'll put some clean clothes in the bedroom for you to use. See you in the morning."

He rushed upstairs to his room and shut the door, leaning back and banging his head against it. God, what a fucking idiot. Why the fuck had he done that? Now he's going to think the only reason I let him stay is for sex. Groaning, he threw himself on his bed and glared at the ceiling.

Idiot. He was an idiot.

Take a Chance

Chapter Ten

Tom woke up early and, after using the bathroom, went downstairs. Seb wasn't up yet, so he had the place to himself. He hadn't slept well, which wasn't surprising after what had happened. He never thought Seb was gay. He'd always had a girlfriend. In fact, it was something Josh had boasted about that his brother was a bit of a stud.

He filled the kettle and put it on while grabbing the other items he needed. Searching the cupboards, he found some bread and popped a couple in the toaster. Again, he thought about last night and that kiss. He could count the number of times he'd kissed on one hand and he'd have fingers left over. It wasn't something he wanted to do with the men he picked up. Why had Seb kissed him if he wasn't gay? Was it something he wanted to do again? Or did Seb think he could kiss him because of what Tom did for a living?

Tom groaned as he leaned against the counter, pinching his lips together. Second guessing it wouldn't help, he needed to speak to him when he got up. No more running away. Ben was right. Maybe it was time for him to take that chance if it was still there for him to do so.

He looked up when he heard a noise coming from upstairs and got another mug out from the cupboard, making coffee for both of them. He put more bread in the toaster and waited for Seb to come downstairs, drumming his fingers on the counter.

Seb walked in, hair sticking up in every direction. Shirtless with his pants hanging dangerously low, he was rubbing his eyes and yawning. He looked up and saw Tom, smiling shyly at him. "Morning."

"Hi. I've made coffee, and there's some toast. You don't mind, do you?"

"What, that you made me breakfast? Fuck no. It's been a long time since that's happened." He walked over and picked up the mug, inhaling its rich aroma before taking a sip. "I needed this," he murmured.

Tom buttered the toast and put some on a plate for him. "Here, have this."

"Thanks."

Tom picked up his plate and mug and walked into the lounge and sat on the sofa. He watched Seb eat his toast, wondering how he was going to approach him about last night when Seb did it for him.

"About last night--"

Tom interrupted, "It's alright, really. You don't have to explain." He suddenly didn't want to hear any excuses that Seb might have. He didn't want to hear Seb tell him that it had been a mistake and had meant nothing. He realised he wanted the kiss to mean something.

"No, I don't want you to think I only asked you to stay so I could make a pass at you."

Tom frowned and tilted his head. "So...ya didn't mean to make a pass at me? Er, alright." He gripped the mug in his hands. So, Seb thought it was a mistake. Great. Just great.

"Alright? What, you're alright with it? I haven't ruined it?" Seb asked him hopefully.

"Ruined what?" Tom shook his head. "I'm just confused as to why it happened that is all. I mean, I know you're not gay, so I'm not sure why ya would kiss me."

"Not gay?" Now it was Seb's turn to frown.

"Yeah, all the time I've known you, you always had a girl on your arm. Josh was always goin' on about your latest conquest. So, yeah, I'm just surprised you kissed me."

"I've dated men and women, Tom, but I just haven't told my parents or Josh about the men. You saw how they reacted to you. I mean, I know they made the odd comment here and there, but when I went there the other day and mentioned seeing you, the things they said..." He shook his head, the disbelief clearly showing on his face. "I was shocked. I've never known them be that way."

"You've dated men?" Tom gasped, eyes wide as he stared at Seb. What? When? Seb had dated men? "Really? You've dated men?"

"Yes." Tom sat back in his seat, mouth hanging open, continuing to stare at Seb. "You know the day your parents kicked you out?" He seemed to wait for Tom, so he nodded, and Seb continued. "They were talking about it when I got home. Obviously, I heard the pregnancy tale, but I couldn't believe they would let you walk out. I ended up having a huge fight with my parents. Now I know why, but back then, I couldn't understand it." He paused while he took a sip of his coffee. "So, I stormed out to look for you. I went everywhere I knew you and Josh hung out but couldn't find you, and eventually I went back home. I walked straight into another fight." He shrugged.

"You looked for me? I didn't think anyone was bothered."

"You were fifteen, Tom. Of course I was bothered. Hell, any sane adult would have been bothered." Seb sighed as he rubbed his neck

"But you were the only one who looked for me. We didn't really know each other. You were Josh's older brother. We only talked when ya were home from Uni."

Tom sat and stared at Seb, who couldn't seem to look him in the eye. What was he thinking? Seb sighed and ran his hand through his hair before he rubbed it over his face.

"You were fourteen, and I was home for the summer. You and Josh were messing in the driveway, cleaning dad's car. Wet." He looked away, seemingly uncomfortable revealing this, but continued. "I remember looking at you, and it was like I was seeing you for the first time. After that, I made a point of coming home more often so that I could spend some time with you. I didn't think anything would come of it. You didn't seem gay." He shrugged and stood up. "Refill?"

"Hang on. Say that again. You liked me? You always had girls. Always! You never... I just didn't know..."

"Yeah, well, you were Josh's mate, and I didn't want to ruin your friendship and like I said, you didn't seem gay."

Tom also stood, clenching his fists as he gritted his teeth. Was this some sick joke? Was Seb taking the piss out of him? Seb wasn't gay, so why was he doing this? Why was he saying he was attracted to him? And if he was, why was he telling him now? Did he think he could get a free fuck out of him now he knew he was gay and a prostitute? Was that why he was being nice to him? The lying shit.

"You expect me to believe that? Is this why you're being nice now? Huh. You must be thanking your lucky stars that I'm a whore. An easy fuckin' lay. Say some kind words, say that ya fancied me and offer me a bed for a night or two. What d'you want, Seb? A free lay? For how long? And what happens to me when ya finished? Back on the streets without another thought? Well, fuck you! Why ya lying to me?"

Seb stared in shock at Tom. "It isn't like that!" Seb said. "That's not why I told you!" Tom started to walk away, only to have Seb grab his arm and spin him back around to face him. "Don't walk away! I thought about telling you last night, but I was scared that this would be how you would react. I just wanted to be honest with you. You were gone for so long and when I saw you again--"

"You what?" Tom interrupted.

"I felt sick, alright. I couldn't stand the thought of you doing that, and you wouldn't let me near you. I've told you this. You ran off, remember?"

"Course I ran off! My fucked up past was staring in my fuckin' face, and the look on your face was priceless, fuckin' priceless. You looked like ya were gonna fuckin' puke. So yeah, I ran."

"And you're going to leave now? Rather than stay and work this out? Yeah, of course you are because it's worked out so well for you in the past," Seb said sarcastically to him.

Tom suddenly grabbed hold of his shirt, screaming in his face. "Fuck off!" He raised a fist to punch Seb when he suddenly pushed him away. Tom spun around and stalked over to the chair, taking deep breaths. He turned back to him. "Why do you care? What does it matter to you?"

Tom watched as Seb sat down on the sofa and dropped his head in his hands. "What can I say, Tom? What can I say to make you see that I want to help you? Sure, I'm attracted to you. That hasn't changed even though I haven't seen you in years." Seb paused, staring at Tom. "I just want to help you. You...you're so much better than this, but I don't want to be fighting with you every step of the way. I guess the question is, why won't you let me help you?"

"And you won't want anything in return?"

"Is it so hard to believe that a friend would want to help you?" he asked with a heavy sigh.

"It's what you'll want in return. Everyone always wants something."

"For fuck's sake, Tom, how many times do I have to say that I don't want anything, well, except getting you off the streets? I won't try anything. I know you don't like me that way."

Tom snorted. "Yeah, wasn't like I kissed ya back, was it?"

"Yeah." Seb gave a small smile. "Look, I don't want to fight with you. Won't you just let me in, let me help?"

Tom stared at Seb for a couple of minutes, thinking about what Seb was offering him. Should he take that chance and trust Seb? His hands were clammy, and he could feel his heart hammering in his chest. What if Seb treated him the way his parents had? What if Seb threw him away too? He couldn't go through that again. He didn't think he could survive it.

Clearing his throat, Tom said, "You've got to understand. I haven't trusted any fucker in a long time, and the people I did trust didn't want to know me once they knew I was gay. I'm not gonna be able to change that overnight."

"I understand, but do you want my help?" Tom slowly nodded his head. "Will you spend the weekend, so we can try to sort something out?"

Again, Tom stared at him before looking away. "Yeah, yeah I'll stay." Dropping his shoulders, Tom sighed, closing his eyes.

"So, how about we get ready and go out? Do something with our day. Get to know each other again. What do you think?"

"Yeah, alright." Tom nodded in agreement.

"Want to borrow some clothes? I think mine might be a bit warmer."

Tom fidgeted on the spot, rubbing the back of his neck as his face grew warm. He was embarrassed by the state of his clothes, but he knew he couldn't keep going out in this weather in the ones he owned. Tom eventually nodded. "Okay, and thanks."

"Great, I'll leave them in your room. There's only a couple of inches difference between us, so they should be alright for you."

Tom went into the bathroom to freshen up, and when he walked into the bedroom, he found the clothes Seb had put out for him. He quickly dressed, realising just how threadbare his were. He felt warm wearing them, and he hadn't felt warm wearing clothes in a long time.

Jogging downstairs, he found Seb in the kitchen, who looked up at him when he entered. "Ready?" Tom nodded. "Okay, I thought we'd get the bus, and then if you want, we can have a drink while we're out."

"Sure, yeah." Smiling, Tom followed Seb to the front door.

Seb chuckled. "I much prefer it when you agree. Come on, the bus will be here soon."

They left the house, Seb locking up behind them, and walked to the bus stop. As they approached, they saw the bus coming up behind them and had to run to make it on time. Once Seb had paid, they sat down, looked at each other and laughed.

"I always had to run for the bus when I was younger. I always wanted to spend another five minutes in bed. I just couldn't get up. My parents were always shouting at me." Seb laughed.

"Yeah, me too. It was like the mattress was glued to my back, especially on cold days, under the blankets all nice and warm."

It was twenty minutes and numerous stops later before they pulled up into the bus station and queued to get off the bus. "Right, where to first?" Seb asked as they walked out. "We're near the Arndale if you want to go there?"

"I'll leave that up to you. I don't go out to town, doesn't seem much point, ya know. When you've got no money, why torture yourself looking at things you can't buy."

Seb looked at him and frowned before nodding. "Yeah, I can understand that, but you can today."

"What?" Tom frowned.

"You need some clothes. The ones you've got have seen better days, right? And don't argue with me. I'm not talking a whole new wardrobe, but you need some new jeans and jumpers to keep you warm. Don't think I haven't noticed how cold you are when you're wearing them. So come on, just accept them. You can even call them an early Christmas present," Seb added cheekily.

"No, it's okay, but thanks. You've done enough."

"Come on. When was the last time someone bought you anything? Let me do this for you. Please." Seb fluttered his eyelashes at Tom.

Tom smiled and agreed, "Alright, thank you."

"I definitely like it when you agree with me. That's what friends are for. Now, let's shop!"

Tom was dragged into so many different shops that they soon seemed to blur into one. Seb appeared genuinely happy to be doing this for him, laughing and joking while making him try different items on. Seb bought him a couple of pairs of jeans and jumpers and a long-sleeved shirt he'd seen him staring at. He had to put a stop when he tried to get him to wear a Christmas jumper though.

"No, not a chance."

"Aww, why not. Bet you look cute in it."

"Cute my arse. Again, no chance."

"Why?"

Tom gaped at him. "Don't you remember? My parents made me wear one every year, one, I might add, that my mum had knitted. I still have nightmares about the one that supposedly had dancing snowmen on the front, but they actually looked like they were fuckin'. The excuses I had to make so I could avoid wearing it. My mum couldn't understand why I wouldn't put it on." Tom shook his head.

Seb threw his head back and burst out laughing. "Oh, I wish I had seen that one. Bet you looked so adorable in it." He patted his cheeks.

"Fuck off, you're not funny." He pouted at him, sticking his bottom lip out.

"Oh I am, I so am," he stated while still chuckling away. "Fucking snowmen," he muttered as he started walking. "Hungry?"

Tom nodded. He was starving. "Yeah."

"Pizza? There's one not far from here."

They both walked towards it while manoeuvring through the crowds of people out shopping. It was only a couple of weeks away from Christmas, so there were lots of people rushing about buying gifts.

When they entered, they had to wait to get a seat, and once they did, they ordered quickly. The place was crowded, and they had to lean over the table so they could hear each other. Tom had noticed how Seb had kept their conversations to safe topics. He was talking about his job, how Uni had gone, the friends he had made and what they were doing now. At no point did he make Tom feel like he shouldn't be there, that he didn't want his company. He'd made him laugh to the point where he had been crying, and he remembered that about him. Seb always made people happy, always had them laughing.

Their food arrived, and they ate quickly, and before long, it was time to leave. Seb paid, and they had to push past people so they could leave. "Man, it was busy in there. Guess it's the Christmas rush, can you imagine what it'll be like next week?" Seb commented as they walked out. He turned to Tom. "Where now?"

Tom groaned. "I'm full, and I think I'm shopped out. I thought all men hated shopping, but you seem to enjoy it."

"Nope, hate it like the next man, but I like getting something for you." He smiled shyly and looked embarrassed as his cheeks flushed.

"Thanks, I've had a good day. And thanks for the clothes."

"Well, what else do you need? Toiletries, er, toothbrush, shoes? Oh my God, you need shoes! Come on, let's go get some." He sounded so enthusiastic that Tom laughed while shaking his head.

"No, seriously, you've bought enough."

"What have you got on your feet, huh? Trainers. You need proper boots in this weather. No arguing!" Seb advised, waggling his finger at him.

Tom stared at him and started laughing. "I don't remember you being so bossy!"

"Boots and socks, this way," Seb told him as he grabbed his arm and dragged in the direction of the shops.

Following Seb as he manoeuvred his way through the crowded streets, they walked into a shoe shop, and it wasn't long before Tom was the owner of an awesome pair of boots and thick socks. He decided to wear them so had his trainers bagged up to go. Seb was right. His feet did feel much warmer.

"We'll stop off at the supermarket and grab some food for tonight. What d'you fancy cooking?"

Tom felt his cheeks heat and he looked away. He couldn't cook.

His parents had never taught him. His mum had always told him it was a woman's job to cook and clean. Some of what he was feeling must have shown on his face because Seb gave him an understanding look and a small smile.

"Guess we'll have a cooking lesson." Seb turned to walk away. Tom reached out and grabbed Seb's hand to thank him. Seb twisted his fingers through Tom's and started walking again, holding his hand. Tom stared down at their joined hands as he walked beside him. Was this the first time someone had held his hand? He couldn't remember a time before. He'd probably had done to him every sexual act going, but something so small and simple as holding hands left him deeply moved and close to tears. Seb hadn't noticed how affected he was and carried on talking to him as if nothing was wrong.

"Something simple then. Pasta, I think. We can pick up the pasta and sauce and some veg to chuck in. Garlic bread too. Wine or beer? Tom? Tom?"

"Sorry. What?" Tom looked up at Seb.

"You okay?"

Tom swallowed, looked down at their joined hands before glancing back up at him and smiling. "Yeah. Sorry, what were you saying?"

Seb looked at him intently like he was trying to see inside his mind and figure out what was going on with him. He looked down at their joined hands. "Too much?"

"What? No, fuck no...Not at all."

"Then what is it? Please don't hide."

Tom looked away, fidgeting and unsure how to answer that question without bringing up what he did. He sighed before answering, "I've never held hands with someone before."

"Never?"

"No. It kinda reminded me of the other thing."

"You mean what you do?"

"Yeah."

Seb nodded but didn't say anything further. They started walking again until they reached the bus stop, standing there in silence. Once the bus came, Seb handed over their tickets and they sat down on an empty seat.

He sighed and closed his eyes. He shouldn't have mentioned it. They'd been having a great day and, for once, he'd forgotten all about what he did and the reasons why. He glanced at Seb, who was staring out the window, and wondered what he could say to make things better again. As if reading his mind, Seb turned to him and smiled, reaching for his hand and holding it in his lap. That simple act helped to calm Tom.

They got off the bus near the supermarket and bought what they needed as quickly as they could. It was packed inside with people barging past one another to reach whatever bargains they could grab. It seemed there was a pre-Christmas sale on, and everyone was there fighting for the goods. He thought the city centre had been bad! There was still another two weeks before Christmas.

Seb held his hand again as they made the walk back to his. Once inside, Tom put his new clothes in his room and then went to the kitchen, where Seb was putting the food away. Seb turned and smiled at him as he walked in. "Ready to cook?"

Take a Chance

Chapter Eleven

Seb watched as Tom somehow managed to turn the pasta into a gloopy mess...again. He could see that Tom was becoming frustrated with himself by the muttering and slamming of cupboard doors. Seb had tried on several occasions to step in and help, but Tom was adamant he could do it, even though he hadn't cooked before. At the rate he was going, they would need more pasta. After a while, Seb had had enough and spoke to Tom.

"Put the timer on, Tom."

Tom growled. "No. I will do this properly. I don't need a fuckin' ticking egg-shaped device to tell me when it's done. There's a fuckin' clock on the wall for that!" He waved a hand in the general direction of the clock and continued to pour more pasta into the pan, covering it with boiling water. Why he'd added more pasta was beyond Seb. If Tom didn't finish cooking soon though, Seb was going to be starving, and he would be ordering take out. He stared at his phone and scratched his chin as he thought about what he would be ordering.

"Don't even think it, Seb," Tom muttered darkly at him, watching him with a frown on his face. "I'll do it this time."

Seb looked at the soggy vegetables and pasta sauce, now sticking to the pan looking like it would need to be soaked off. It didn't look fit for human consumption. He sighed and told himself that Tom was trying, and this was his first attempt. Maybe pasta was too hard for a first try. Soup. Yeah, he should have gone with soup. What could go wrong with that?

"Fuck, fuck, fuck! It's goin' funny again."

Seb reached over and turned the gas off, grabbing the colander and pan. "It'll have to do, 'cause I'm starving." Emptying the pan of pasta, he quickly rinsed it and mixed it with the sauce. It didn't look good. Not good at all. He swallowed hard as his stomach rolled and he continued to mix the pasta and sauce together. Seb didn't feel hungry now, but for Tom's sake, he would try.

"Pass me the plates, please."

The plates appeared in front of him and he served the pasta, putting a slice of garlic bread with it. At least the bread looked edible. Walking into the lounge, he sat down and tried to find some interest in the food in front of him.

"If I said I wasn't hungry, would ya kill me?" Tom asked.

Seb looked at Tom, who was frowning at his plate, pushing the food around it. He looked back at his own plate. "Chinese?"

The look of relief on Tom's face said it all. "Thank fuck for that. Yeah, fuck yeah."

Seb laughed. "You'll do better next time."

Tom gaped at him. "You want me to cook again? Are you mad?"

"We all make mistakes at first," Seb told him.

"There's making mistakes, and then there's giving someone food poisoning! I wouldn't give this to a dog!" Tom pointed at the food on the plate.

Laughing, Seb stood up and took the plates into the kitchen before ordering the Chinese. His stomach turned over as he scraped the plates clean, swallowing as the clumpy food slid from the plates. Thank God they hadn't eaten it.

Seb cleaned up the kitchen as he waited for their food order to arrive, noticing that somehow all the pans appeared to have been used, and all looked black with burnt food stuck to them. How had Tom managed it? Seb tried to scrub at one particular spot that didn't want to come clean, grunting at the effort needed.

"Er, shouldn't I be doing that?" Tom asked, rubbing the back of his neck.

"I think they need to soak for a while longer, like maybe a week."

"Ha, fuckin', ha," Tom muttered sarcastically. "Don't forget, I did warn ya."

Smirking, Seb left the pots in the sink and reached to get clean plates out. "Food should be here soon."

"I'll pretend not to notice how relieved ya seem about that."

"I'm going to persevere. You will learn to cook." Seb put the plates on the counter.

"Well, I hope your life insurance is up to date because I won't be eating anything I cook anytime soon," Tom muttered darkly at him, narrowing his eyes.

The doorbell rang, and Seb went to pay for the food. It didn't take long for them to dish it out and sit down to eat. Seb moaned as the food hit his taste buds. "So good," he mumbled with a mouth full of food.

"Yeah, yeah," Tom muttered, while shovelling food into his own mouth.

"Come on, don't be like that. When I first learned to cook, I thought Mum was going to kill me. I burnt everything, and I swear she tried to whack me with her favourite frying pan when she'd seen that I had managed to burn chocolate on it."

Tom laughed. "On yeah, I remember Josh telling me some shit about you and cooking. Isn't that the reason your mum never bothered to teach him?"

"Yeah, I scarred her for life, but at least I can cook now."

Once they'd finished and cleared everything away, Seb suggested another movie with popcorn and they both settled on the sofa. Seb smiled to himself. Tom had chosen to sit near him instead of on the chair. He inched his way closer until he was next to him. He felt Tom stiffen slightly. "Is this alright with you?"

Tom ducked his head, but not before Seb detected the slight blush on his cheeks. He turned and looked at him and smiled shyly. "Yeah. It's fine."

"You sure?"

Tom nodded. "Yeah. It's nice," he said picking at some invisible lint on his jeans.

Seb put his arm around him, watching for any reactions that would tell him to back off. Again, Tom looked shy and a little unsure. For a man with as much sexual experience as him, it appeared that small, innocent touches made him blush.

"Can I ask you something?"

Tom turned to look at him, his face close. Seb looked down at his lips then back up to stare into his blue eyes. Tom hadn't missed that look if the flushed cheeks were anything to go by. "Yeah."

"Have you ever had someone, you know, like a boyfriend?"

Tom looked away. "No. I'd just finally come to terms with my sexuality when all the shit hit the fan, and I don't like the thought of kissing a punter." He shrugged before continuing, "I told you earlier that that was the first time I'd held someone's hand."

"What was your first time like? You don't have to tell me if you don't want to," Seb added quickly when he felt Tom tense up.

"It was painful and rushed. It was my first job, the first guy. I didn't know anything about doing it. I had condoms but didn't know about prep, not that it matters. He pulled over, asked how much, and I got into his car. He drove to an alley, and I got into the back seat. It was over quickly, and I left. I felt used and swore I wouldn't do it again, but I had no choice."

"I'm so sorry."

Tom smiled at him. "Don't apologise for something that wasn't your fault." Taking a deep breath, he continued. "First couple of months it was like that. Giving blow jobs and getting fucked, and then some other kid saw me, offered to buy me a drink. I was cold, hungry and sore. I accepted, and he told me how I could work it. If I gave a blow job, always use a condom and don't fuck anyone unless I need to. He told me to be upfront from the start as to what I would be willing to do. It worked. I don't have to let someone fuck me unless I need the money." Tom paused before whispering, "I'm used to it now."

Before he could stop himself, Seb leaned over and kissed Tom gently, keeping the touch light, trying to offer him some comfort. When Tom didn't back away, Seb kissed him again, moving over Tom's lips and across his jaw. He felt Tom suck in a breath before he turned his head, seeking Seb's lips.

They kissed again, harder this time, and Seb held his face in his hands as he deepened the kiss. He ran his tongue across Tom's bottom lip before biting it gently.

Tom opened his mouth with a moan, and Seb took advantage, sweeping his tongue in so it could tangle with Tom's. He felt Tom grab his shoulders and pull him closer, wanting more contact. Seb leaned over him until they were lying on the sofa with Seb on top. He could feel how hard Tom was as he pushed his groin up, rubbing against his hip.

Seb groaned and moved until he was rubbing both their erections together, lying between Tom's legs. They moved together and Seb could feel himself getting lost in the sensations. He groaned again and moved away, putting some space between them. Things were going too fast, and Seb could feel how close he was to coming. Tom leaned up and continued to kiss his throat causing Seb to moan. "Stop, Tom."

Tom opened his eyes and looked at him, his pupils dilated and lust blazing from his eyes. "Why?"

"Because I don't want to rush this, and I almost came in my pants." He looked away as he felt his cheeks heat up.

Tom smiled at him brightly. "Yeah?"

Seb laughed. "Yeah. You don't have to look so happy about it."

"So...no more making out then?" Tom stuck his lip out a little.

"I didn't say that!"

Tom laughed. "Good. I like kissing you." He leaned up to kiss him again.

Seb kissed him back, feeling the passion build quickly between them again. Slowing the kisses, he reached up to touch Tom's cheek before pulling away. He smiled at him, noticing the flushed cheeks and the slight panting coming from him. "Beer?" he asked.

"Fuck, you're asking now?" Tom asked him, eyes going wide.

Take a Chance

"Yeah. Beer, movie, making out on the sofa. What could be better?"

Tom smiled. "I like that."

They spent the rest of the evening doing exactly that before clearing up and going to bed. Seb stood outside the bedroom door, kissing Tom.

"Goodnight." He smiled. "I'll see you in the morning."

Tom kissed him back, and Seb could feel him smiling against his lips. "Night."

Tom turned and closed the bedroom door behind him, and Seb walked into his room and also closed the door. Leaning back against it, he smiled to himself. They'd had such a good day together, and there'd only been a couple of instances of awkwardness between them and Tom hadn't felt the need to leave and do the other stuff.

Getting undressed, he palmed his hard dick and stroked it slowly as he remembered how Tom had felt beneath him. Within seconds, he was coming and had to shove his fist in his mouth to muffle the moans. Once he cleaned up, he climbed into bed and fell asleep, thinking of Tom.

❋ ❋ ❋

Tom woke the next day feeling better than he had in a long time. He couldn't recall the last time he felt so light, like he might have something to look forward to, something good in his life. Like he didn't have the weight of the world on his shoulders. Maybe he wasn't the failure he thought he was.

Yesterday had simply been one of the best days he'd had in years.

It had felt so easy, so comfortable spending time with Seb, holding his hand and making out on the sofa. The fact that Seb didn't try to make any moves on him and kept it to just kissing made him feel strangely clean and like he might mean something to Seb. He didn't understand it, and he couldn't explain it, but being with Seb like that the night before had made him feel better about himself. Made him feel like he wasn't the stain he thought he was.

Tom lay listening to the sounds of the house, but he couldn't hear Seb moving around, so assumed he was still in bed until he heard a knock on his door.

"Yeah," he called through the closed door, smiling to himself.

The door opened, and Seb stuck his head in and smiled at him. "Can I come in?"

Tom nodded and patted the bed as Seb walked over to him, carrying two mugs. He put them on the bedside cabinet before he pulled the covers up and slid into bed next to him.

"Did you sleep alright?"

Tom nodded again. "Yeah. I did."

"I've been awake for a while, wondering if I should come in and see if you were awake." Seb gave him a small smile.

Tom rolled onto his side, facing Seb and smiled at him. Seb copied the action, and they lay facing each other. Seb reached over and touched his face with his fingers before leaning over him and kissing him on his lips.

Tom pulled away, making a face. "Morning breath."

Seb smiled, sat up and reached over to pass Tom the mug. He drank some tea before handing it back. He'd wanted to wake up next to Seb, but was glad in a way that he hadn't. He liked the fact that Seb didn't want to rush anything, but he was worried the reason was that he was a whore. He'd probably had more sex with strangers than he'd had hot meals.

Seb smiled at him and leaned over to kiss him again, pulling him close and wrapping an arm around his waist and pushing his leg in between Tom's.

Tom opened his mouth and felt Seb's tongue touch his. He moaned softly at the contact and moved his hips towards Seb's, feeling Seb's erection rub against his own. They both only had boxers on, and Tom wanted to push his hand into Seb's, so he could touch him and make him come.

Seb rolled on top of him and continued to kiss him, rubbing their dicks together. He groaned as he continued to rub against Seb. It wouldn't be long until he came if they carried on. Then he felt Seb's hand stroking him through his boxers, and he groaned again. "God yes, please touch me."

Seb pushed Tom's boxers down over his hips and curled his fingers around Tom's cock. "God, you feel good." He slowly stroked him, then moved his thumb over the head, smearing the precome around, making him wet. Tom couldn't stop his hips thrusting forward, pushing his cock through Seb's fist. Seb tightened his grip on him and stroked him faster.

Tom moaned into the kiss, pushing his tongue into Seb's mouth. Feelings overwhelmed him. Someone else was touching him, wanting him to feel good. He squeezed his eyes closed, gasping as his balls pulled up. Lightning ran through him and Tom shuddered beneath Seb.

"Oh, fuck, fuck!" He groaned as he came, spilling thick and hot over Seb's fist. His body shuddered, and he lay gasping when he'd stopped coming. Seb continued stroking him through his orgasm, kissing him gently before releasing him and wiping his hands on his own boxers.

Tom slowly opened his eyes and looked up at Seb. He reached down to touch Seb, but Seb stopped him. "No. That was for you." He leaned down and kissed him again. "Stay here and I'll make us some breakfast. Toast, alright?"

"Yeah. I think I like waking up to this in the mornings. An orgasm followed by breakfast in bed."

"Yeah, yeah. Don't get used to it." Seb pulled back the covers and got out, standing and stretching. Tom looked him over and admired what he saw. He could see that Seb worked out. He wasn't overly muscled, but he was in shape with a nice six pack. Damn, he looked good! Tom smiled as he watched Seb leave the room, staring at his arse the entire time.

Tom lay in bed and listened to the sounds Seb made as he made breakfast in the kitchen. He could get up, have a quick shower and brush his teeth by the time Seb came back upstairs. He was in definite need of a shower now. He felt a little itchy as the come Seb hadn't caught dried on his skin. He threw back the covers and walked to the bathroom.

A few minutes later, Tom left the bathroom and entered the bedroom to find Seb in bed waiting for him. Seb pulled back the covers. "Get back in here." Tom hesitated. He only had a towel wrapped around his hips.

"Want me to close my eyes?" Seb wriggled his eyebrows at him.

"Ha, fuckin', ha." Mind made up, Tom dropped his towel and walked over to the bed, making sure Seb got a good look. Tom could see that Seb liked what he saw. His mouth was open slightly and he seemed to be breathing a little quicker. Tom leaned over him as he crawled into bed. Yeah, he liked what he saw. His pupils had dilated, and there was a slight flush on his cheeks.

"Tea and toast in bed. I think the last person who did this for me

Take a Chance

was me mum. Thanks." He smiled sweetly at him, outwardly ignoring Seb's obvious arousal, but inside he was doing a happy dance. He knew he was thin, that he needed to put on some weight, but the look Seb gave him, well yeah, it made him feel good.

"Er, yeah. Eat it up before it goes cold." He seemed to hesitate before continuing. "I need to go to my parents today for lunch, but you can stay here if you want." Seb looked at him as he spoke.

"Thanks, but I can't. I need to get back and see how the others are. I've not seen them since Friday."

"Will you be coming back later? I can cook us some tea."

"You sure?" Tom asked. He didn't want to overstay his welcome.

"Absolutely." Seb touched Tom's hand.

Tom smiled at him. He felt like his face would split with how wide his smile was. He wasn't alone in this, whatever this was between them. Who would have thought they would be here together like this when he ran away from Seb that first night?

"Are you gonna tell your parents?"

"You mean about us?" Tom nodded at Seb's question. "No, I really don't think that's wise, and it's not because I'm ashamed of you. Never think that, but after the last time I mentioned your name, let's just say it's best not to go there."

"Oh, okay." Tom's shoulders dropped, and he glanced away wincing. Part of him was hoping Seb would tell his parents about them, even if this thing between them had only just started. But, he understood why Seb would be hesitant in telling his parents. Who would want to tell their parents they were involved with a whore?

"No, it's not okay. I want to tell them about us, but this thing between us has just begun, and we need to talk about what we want and how we're going to work and I don't want my parent's homophobia to ruin us. I want to give us a chance. I don't want to have them destroy us."

"Is it because of what I do?"

"Partly, but also where you live. How could I feel comfortable here in my home, knowing you're in an abandoned house with no gas or electricity? I'd be here nice and warm and comfortable and you wouldn't. Do you understand what I'm trying to say?"

Thinking about what Seb had said, Tom could see that Seb was right. If the situation was reversed he wouldn't be happy with Seb working on the streets and living in some shitty hovel trying to survive. But Tom didn't have anything else, and he didn't want to sponge off Seb, taking handouts. Wouldn't he still be getting paid for sex? The situation would be different, but the result would still be the same.

"Yeah, I get it. I'll meet you back here later. What time's best for you?"

"Anytime after three. Now eat up."

After finishing breakfast, Seb went to his room and dressed to go to his parents while Tom did the same. It wasn't long before they were both ready to go.

As he stood by the door, Tom suddenly felt awkward. Should he kiss Seb goodbye or just wave or some other shit? Deciding to play it safe he gave a casual wave as he started to walk down the drive. Seb frowned at him and then shook his head.

"What do you think you're doing?"

"Er, leaving?" Tom frowned at Seb.

"Tell me where you live and I'll drop you off."

Tom instantly tensed, muscles rigid. He didn't want Seb to know where he lived, to see the condition of the house. "Nah, it's alright. I'll

Take a Chance

walk, but thanks anyway."

Seb looked at him, and then opened the passenger side door. "In."

When Tom didn't make a move towards the door, Seb sighed. "I know the conditions you live in, you told me."

"Yeah, it's one thing to be told about it but another to fuckin' see it."

"Just get in. It'll be quicker if I drop you off unless you've got some more excuses."

"Excuses? I'm not making up any fuckin' excuses." Tom put his hands on his hips.

Seb sighed and shook his head. "Please just get in the car."

Yes, he was finding excuses. Seb was right on that. Tom glanced away, scuffing his boot on the ground. Why he was so hesitant to let Seb take him home?

Being honest with himself, having spent the weekend at Seb's house, he wasn't looking forward to going back to where he lived. The cold and dampness of the house. The condition of the place. He stood looking at Seb, who was waiting patiently by the car door, maintaining eye contact with him. Tom sighed and finally walked over and got in the car, giving Seb the address.

As Seb drove, Tom was silent, watching the scenery and preparing himself for going back into that house. He didn't want Seb to see the house, didn't want him to see the conditions he lived in. He tapped his fingers on the window frame as his knee bounced, looking out the window at the houses as they passed. Too soon, they were turning into his street. "Just drop me off here," Tom said to Seb.

Seb pulled over and looked down the street. There were plenty of run down properties in the area. People didn't have the money to do the houses up in the current economy.

Seb turned to him. "I'll see you later, alright?"

"Yeah." He hesitated before opening the door.

"Hey."

He looked back as Seb leaned over him and kissed him. "Later."

Tom got out of the car and stood on the pavement watching Seb drive away. Sighing, he walked slowly towards the alley. He didn't want to go back there.

Take a Chance

Chapter Twelve

Tom walked into the house and immediately found Ben pacing the lounge and waving his hands. "What's wrong?"

"Adam's missing."

What? "Fuck. How? I thought he would've been out with you?" Tom stared at Ben as Ben gripped his hair.

"We had a stupid fuckin' argument. I tried talking to him about some of the risks he's been taking, but he wouldn't listen to me. Told me to fuck off and not bother him again and then he left. I waited a few minutes to let him calm down then went to where he said he was goin', but he wasn't there. I checked all the places we go, *all of them*, and I couldn't find him anywhere. I've asked people but no one's seen him."

Ben slumped to the floor, his face losing all colour. His lips trembled, and Tom rushed over to him, kneeling before him, reaching out to grip his shoulder.

"So he's been missing since last night then?" Tom asked as calmly as he could.

Ben shook his head. "No, Friday."

"Friday? Fuck." That was almost two days ago. "No sign of him anywhere?"

Ben shook his head again. "I'm gonna go to the cops. I know they won't take it seriously. I mean, we're prostitutes, right? So why would they care, but I've got to try. Fuck! This is my entire fault. If I hadn't argued with him, if I had just dropped it, he wouldn't have left the way he did, and I would've been there to watch his back. If anything happens to him--"

"Nothing will have happened to him, so don't go blaming yourself. You said it yourself that he was taking more risks. That he wasn't watching out like he should've been." Tom glanced down before looking back up at Ben. "We'll find him. Tell me where you've been looking."

They sat on the floor as Ben told him all the areas he had searched. Tom chewed his lip as he listened to Ben swallowing in an attempt to moisten his dry mouth. Adam had never been gone this long before. He'd always returned the next day.

As they made plans to search other areas, Matt and Luke came in. They'd also been out searching but hadn't seen anything. Luke slumped on the floor, looking exhausted with dark bags under his eyes. Matt didn't look much better.

"We spoke to some of the people there, but no one's seen him in a few days," Matt advised. "So it looks like he was picked up fairly quickly on Friday and didn't make it back to any of his regular haunts."

Luke nodded his agreement. "People are worried. One of the girls went missing Wednesday. The police know about it, and they aren't doing much, but then again, they don't have that much to go on. She wasn't working with anyone. The only way we know about it is that she told one of the other girls where she was going that night."

"Shit. Let's try looking again while we've got some daylight, hit the same areas again. Maybe someone else will be out who might have seen something. It beats sitting here and waiting," Tom commented as he stood.

"I'll stay here, just in case he does come back," Ben advised staying sat on the floor.

Tom looked down at him and nodded, understanding that Ben needed to be alone right now. He was blaming himself for the situation, even though it wasn't his fault. He'd only been looking out for his friend. If it was anyone's fault, then it was Adam's for being reckless.

Matt and Luke headed out and Tom went to some of the areas he knew Adam frequented. After speaking to some of the people working there, Tom quickly realised he was getting the same answer. No one had seen Adam for a few days, and everyone was on edge.

Damn, they wouldn't be in this position if he had stayed Friday. Tom might have been able to talk some sense into Adam if he had been there with Ben. But no, he had to go to Seb's to apologise. If only he hadn't taken that money. He looked up to the sky, realising that more time had passed than he'd thought. It was starting to get dark, and he wouldn't be able to keep looking once the light went. There was only so much you could do when it was dark.

Unless you had a car.

Thinking about a car immediately brought Seb to mind again. Tom could head over there and ask him for help. Knowing the kind of person Seb was, he knew he wouldn't say no.

It took him almost thirty minutes to get there, and he was relieved to see his car on the drive. Knocking on the door, he waited for him to answer as he paced in front of the door, running a hand through his long hair.

As soon as the door opened, he started talking. "Seb, I need your help. Adam's gone missing, and no one's seen him since Friday. Can we use your car to search for him? Please."

Seb looked at him, blinking rapidly for a few seconds before he nodded. "Yeah, come in while I grab my keys and coat. Where does he usually go?"

"We've tried the usual places, so I'm not sure. We could try them again?" Tom followed Seb into the hallway, watching Seb put his trainers on.

"What about places he used to go but doesn't now?"

Tom thought for a few seconds. Adam had previously used some of the old abandoned warehouses but hadn't gone there for some time now. The people who hung out there drank a lot and did drugs, and Adam had explained that he didn't want to get involved in that. They had all seen what that could do to people.

"The factory buildings in the older part of the city. He used to go there a while back, but drunks and drug users are there. Not a safe place, but he wouldn't have gone back there."

Tom followed Seb out of the house, and then they both got into Seb's car, and he started driving.

"I thought that area was being regenerated and that the police had moved people on." Seb commented driving towards the area Tom had mentioned.

"Some of it fell through, and some of the other buildings need knocking down."

They sat in silence while Seb drove. Tom couldn't stop fidgeting, and he had to keep taking deep breaths and swallowing in an attempt to stop himself from being sick. Would they find anything? Or was it a waste of time? Tom became aware of Seb slowing down and realised they were almost there. The road was full of potholes that needed filling and Seb was driving carefully to try and avoid the worst ones. Lamp posts were either out or broken, and the whole area was dark. It wasn't long before Seb pulled up.

"We're here. Come on." Seb undid his seatbelt and opened the car door.

Getting out of the car, Tom glanced around the area. It was easy to see how dilapidated the area had become. Parts of the broken pavement had weeds growing through the cracks, and there was rubbish scattered around. Bin bags were piled up, and Tom could see needles in the waste.

The warehouse had been empty for some time. The windows had been boarded up at some point, but some of the boards were now missing, and the glass had been smashed. The metal frames appeared to be bleeding as the rust ran down the wall. The graffiti covered walls had water running down them from the broken guttering above. Weeds grew everywhere, and there was even a tree attempting to grow from out of the roof.

Tom stared up at the building and swallowed. He closed his eyes briefly as he tried to calm himself. Wiping his clammy hands on his jeans, he scanned the dark area and stepped closer to Seb. He hoped Adam hadn't come here. He turned to look at Seb, who was also staring at the building.

"Doesn't look like a good place to be, right?" Tom muttered. He didn't want to speak too loudly and draw attention to them.

Seb shook his head as he turned to look at him. "When was the last time Adam was here?" Seb also spoke quietly.

"Maybe eight months ago? I'm not sure to be honest. He doesn't talk about himself much."

Seb nodded. "How do we get in?"

"Over there." Tom pointed to the side of the warehouse.

They walked around the outside of the building, stepping over rubbish and broken bricks, and found a door that had been pulled partially away from its frame and hung limply on its side.

They entered the building, and Tom stepped back as the smell hit him. He coughed as it seemed to catch in his throat. Damp, mouldy and a sweet, but rotting odour. The inside looked worse than the outside. Paint hung in strips from the walls and chunks of plaster was also missing. Graffiti covered every surface and at some point the ceiling had partially collapsed, allowing the rain to come in.

Overturned metal racking lay rusting on the floor, piles of paper and cardboard lay scattered about, soggy and mushy-looking. Remains of bedding and fires lay around the area and in between these were puddles that had formed due to the rain water.

Pigeons nested on the rusted metal ceiling support beams, and Tom could hear them cooing softly as their feathers rustled together. He felt that there were a thousand eyes watching him and the hairs on the back of his neck stood up, his skin breaking out in goose bumps. He suddenly felt cold to the bone and shivered as he rubbed his hands up and down his arms.

"Where would he be?" Seb asked, scanning the area.

Tom turned to Seb and pointed to the far corner of the room. "There's a door there that leads to the other rooms. He would have gone to one of those, but it's hard to think that he would come here."

"Are you sure he would have?"

Take a Chance

Tom sighed as he looked around the warehouse again and shook his head. "I don't know, but I can't think of anywhere else and, this is the only place I can remember him mentioning."

They walked across the floor, and Seb pushed the door open. On the other side was a corridor that had several doors leading off of it. Tom went along and checked each room as he passed it, seeing nothing inside but rubbish, clothes and the occasional mattress.

"If people have been living here, then where are they all?" Seb asked as he continued walking.

"I don't know. They could have been moved on by the police 'cause of the regeneration work. A lot of money's being poured into it. But like I said before, some work has already stopped." He turned and went to open a door, but it was jammed shut. Seb came over and helped him to push it open.

The smell hit him immediately, like he'd walked into a wall. A putrid, rotting smell that made him gag the instant he smelled it. Lifting his sleeve to cover his mouth, he looked in and immediately spun around, squeezing his eyes shut in a vain attempt to eradicate the image he had just seen.

Lying on a mattress in the corner of the room was Adam. Naked. Dead.

It looked like he had been beaten and possibly stabbed. It was hard to tell. His body was bloated, with what appeared to be open wounds covering it. His sightless, milky eyes stared at him from across the room.

Staggering out and dropping to his knees, Tom vomited over the floor. Every time he managed to take a breath in, it seemed like he could taste that smell and that caused him to gag again. He crawled further down the corridor and eventually sat down, leaning against the wall. He took a shaky breath in and wiped his mouth on his sleeve, looking back to the room he'd just left. He could hear Seb talking in the background, but couldn't make out what he was saying.

Tom wasn't sure how long he'd sat on the floor until Seb approached him. "Come on. We need to go outside and wait for the police."

Tom nodded but wasn't quite sure what he should be doing. Seb reached down and grabbed his arm, pulling him up from the floor. It was like he was there, but at the same time, he wasn't. Everything seemed so distant. He was aware of Seb helping him to walk and looked up to realise he was outside, but couldn't remember how he'd gotten there. He turned and watched as Seb walked to him, holding something in his hand.

"Here, drink some water, but only take small sips."

He took the bottle from him and looked at it, seeing it shake in his hand. Eventually, Seb took the bottle from him and opened it before handing it back. He drank some water and looked out around the area. In the distance, he could hear sirens that appeared to be getting louder.

"Let's sit in the car. We might be here for a while."

Following Seb on unsteady legs, Tom slowly walked to Seb's car and sat sideways in the passenger seat with his feet on the road. He dropped his head between his knees and took several deep, shuddering breaths in and out. He couldn't get the image out of his mind. Adam. God, what the fuck had happened to him? Had he begged for his life? Had he screamed out for help? Fuck, what had he felt in those last few minutes? Had he known he was going to die?

Tom should have been there. He should have been with them, not with Seb.

Police cars arrived, pulling up near Seb's car outside the warehouse. Officers exited the cars and Tom watched them, detached from it all. It felt like he was watching a film. None of it seemed real.

It was like a nightmare, one he desperately wanted to wake up from. Adam couldn't be dead.

Seb stood with the officers then disappeared inside the warehouse. He eventually returned to the car and squatted down near him. "You doing alright?"

Tom turned to him to say something, but all that came out was a sob followed by more. He couldn't contain them. He felt Seb pull him into his arms, and he wrapped his arms around him and sobbed uncontrollably into his chest. Seb rubbed his back and held him tight as he cried.

After a few minutes, he pulled back and wiped his face with his hand. Seb gave him a small smile. "Better?"

Tom choked out a laugh. "Not really." He looked around noticing an ambulance had arrived, lights flashing. "Are they taking his body to the hospital?"

"No, I don't think so. Crime scene people need to get here and do their thing. Then I think a coroner's van will come, but I'm not sure. The police are going to want to talk to you and take your statement. We'll need to go to the police station. Are you up for that?"

"No, but it needs to be done, right?" Seb nodded. "When do we need to go?"

"I'll go over and find out. Stay in the car where it's warm. You look better than you did before, but you still haven't gotten your colour back."

Tom looked at him and frowned. "Colour back?"

"Yeah, you were a bit pale, but you seem better now. I'll be back in a minute."

Seb walked over and approached an officer. They talked for a few minutes before Seb came back. He got in the car and turned to Tom.

"They'll be here for a while, so someone will come over and take our statements, but we might have to go the station again tomorrow. You alright with that?"

Tom nodded. "I just want to go now. I need to let the others know."

Seb didn't say anything but reached across to grab his hand and hold it tight. They sat in the car and waited for an officer to come over and speak to them. It seemed to take an eternity before an officer came over. They both gave statements and answered a lot of questions and, about an hour later, they were allowed to go. Seb gave contact details for himself, advising the police they could reach both Seb and Tom on them.

As Seb started the drive back to his, Tom spoke. "Can you drop me off at mine? I need to tell the others."

"Yeah. Want me to come with you?"

"No, but thanks."

Seb didn't say anything as he drove back to the street he had dropped Tom before. Tom sat staring out of the window but wasn't paying attention. How was he going to tell them? God, Ben was going to be a mess. He already blamed himself and now to find out Adam was dead?

Tom should have been there. He shouldn't have been with Seb. None of this would have happened if he had stayed where he belonged. If he had been there, he could have talked to Adam, found out what was going on. He could have helped him. Now? Now he was dead, and Tom felt it was his fault. His stomach was like lead, hands shaking as he rubbed his face.

When Seb pulled up, Tom opened the door and got out without speaking. As he walked away, he heard Seb shout to him. "Hey, wait."

Tom stopped and turned to face him. "What?"

Take a Chance

"What? Are you alright? You just got out. You didn't say a word."

"Okay, sorry. Thanks for the lift back. I'll see you around." He started to walk away when he felt his arm grabbed.

"You're just walking away?"

"I said thanks, what more do you fuckin' want?" Tom shrugged Seb's hand off his arm. "Me mate's dead. I should've been here instead of with you and I've got to go in there and tell the others what I saw. I have to go."

Tom walked away, and Seb didn't follow. He slowly walked to the back of the house and stood outside the door, preparing himself. How was he going to tell them?

Chapter Thirteen

Tom walked into to the lounge and found the other three sat on the floor together. Ben jumped up when he saw him and started asking questions.

"He's dead," Tom blurted out and then winced. That wasn't quite how he meant to tell them.

There was a stunned silence, and then questions were fired at him from all three of them.

"How d'you know?"

"Did you find him?"

"Where is he?"

"Do the police know?"

"Stop, stop please." Tom held out his hands in front of them in an attempt to calm them down. "I found him. I went to Seb's, and he drove us to the old warehouses to see if he was there. When--"

"No," Ben interrupting him. "He said he would never go back there."

"That's where we found him, in one of the rooms. He'd been there a couple of days. Seb called the police, and they came. We had to give statements. When we left, Adam was still there."

They all stared at him before Matt whispered, "What happened to him?"

"I don't fuckin' know. He looked like he'd been beaten up--" Tom took in a shuddering breath before continuing-- "and I could see what looked like stab wounds to his chest. He'd been dead a while. Fuck, I need a drink. Have we got anything in?"

Luke pointed to a bottle. "Cider. If you want something else, you'll need to go and buy some."

Tom noticed Ben staring at him, looking him up and down his lips pulled back in a sneer as he clenched his fists.

"Nice clothes, Tom. Where d'you get the money for them? Where were you while Adam was murdered?" Ben shouted at him.

Tom turned and looked at Ben. "What the fuck are you gettin' at?"

"Hey, don't start, not know," Luke jumped in. "This isn't going to help us. He left, remember, you tried to help him, and he screamed at you and ran outta here. It's no one's fault what happened. We all tried to talk to him about how he was risking himself. It was almost like he needed to prove to himself that nothing could happen to him."

"I know what you're saying, Luke, but he--" Ben pointed at Tom-- "he said that he would always be there for us. He said that it was safer to work together and when we needed him, where the fuck was here? Off fuckin' his boyfriend. Does he know? Does he know you let men fuck you for money?"

"You know he does."

Luke stood in front of Ben. "Stop this, it's no one's fault."

Ben pushed past Luke and stood next to Tom, their faces close. "Where were you while we were searching for him?" he shouted, spraying spittle in Tom's face.

Tom looked away unable to look him in the eyes. Ben was right. He hadn't been there.

"Can't look at me, can you? You know I'm fuckin' right." Ben pushed Tom, and he stumbled back.

"Yeah, I should have been here. That's all I've thought about since I fuckin' found him. I feel responsible for what happened to him." Tom faced Ben, but couldn't look him in the face.

Luke stepped in between both of them again. "No, you're not responsible. He made his own choice and you--" Luke turned to face Ben-- "you tried to help him. He wanted to go out. What could Tom have done if he were here? Short of tying him up, neither of you could have done anything. Stop blaming yourselves and each other. Shouting at each other won't bring him back."

Ben grabbed his coat and walked out the room, not saying anything to anyone. Tom sighed and sat leaning against the wall. "Pass me the cider will you, Matt? I need a drink."

Luke squatted in front of him. "Don't blame yourself."

Tom grunted. "He's right. I should have been here."

Luke shook his head and grabbed his chin so he could look him in the eyes. "This Seb, he's a good guy, right?" Tom nodded. "He knows about you?" Tom nodded again. "Then, if you have the chance to get out of this, take it. If any of us have a chance to escape this life, you know we would. Don't feel responsible for something that wasn't your fault."

Luke stood and walked over to Matt, sitting next to him while Tom grabbed the bottle of cider. He needed to get drunk.

❋ ❋ ❋

It had been several days since Seb had seen Tom. Days where he'd had to deal with the police, answer more questions and eventually admit that he didn't know where Tom lived. And he still had to work.

He'd spoken to Fin, keeping him up to date as to what was happening, and Fin had advised him to be patient. But Seb wasn't sure how long he could remain patient for.

On Friday, he was in a meeting with his boss, Geoff, regarding a new client whose case they were taking on when the police called again. He apologetically left the room and after answering more questions, returned, apologising again.

"Sorry about that."

"I take it they're still asking questions about that body you found?"

Seb nodded. "Yeah and it doesn't help that Tom doesn't have a phone, so I can't contact him."

"Why don't you go over to his house?"

Seb looked away. If only it were as simple as that. He sighed before answering. "I don't know exactly where he lives. I know the street but not the house number. It's complicated."

Geoff stared at him. "You don't know where he lives?"

"No, as I said, it's complicated."

"Uncomplicate it for me," Geoff told him in a voice that meant business. "The police have been calling virtually every day, and that's on the days where they haven't shown up. I think I've been lenient with you over this. I know this is your private business, but it's having an effect on your work, so give me something. Please."

Seb looked at him while deciding what he should tell him, if anything at all. He rubbed his hand against his chin before sighing as he looked away, staring out of the window.

"I...it isn't my story to tell."

Geoff nodded, but continued to stare intently at him. "I understand that, I do. But I need something here."

Seb nodded again as he considered what Geoff was asking. Would Geoff look at him differently if he told him the truth? And how would Tom react, knowing someone knew about him and what he'd been forced to do?

Rubbing his hands over his face, Seb leaned forward in his chair, staring at Geoff. "Alright. I'll tell you, but you have to understand the situation. Tom had no choice. He really didn't. If I had known back then, I would have done everything I could to have helped him out, but I didn't know the truth until recently. So hear me out before you decide on anything. Please."

Geoff nodded. "Okay, I take it this isn't going to be pretty, right?"

Seb shook his head. He sighed again before he started telling Geoff. "Tom was someone I knew back when I went to high school and the first couple of years at Uni. He was my brother's best mate. They were like two peas in a pod, you know. They did everything together. Always around each other's houses. Spent every minute together." Seb sighed before continuing, "Then one day Tom disappears, but I was at Uni, so I didn't find out about it until I came back. I searched for him. I mean he was only fifteen at the time. My parents had told me he had gotten some girl pregnant and had done a runner, but that didn't sound like him. He was always responsible, even though he hung out with Josh. Always the sensible one. He worked for his parents as they owned a corner shop. Well, after that there was nothing, no news at all. Things carried on as usual, and he was never mentioned again.

"A few weeks ago I was driving near Canal Street, and there was a group of boys stood hanging around. You know, rent boys. I glanced at them as I drove past, not really paying any attention, but one of them looked familiar."

"Tom."

Seb looked up at him and nodded. "Yeah, Tom."

Seb went on to explain everything that had happened since he'd seen Tom that fateful night. When he'd finished talking, silence filled the room. Eventually Geoff spoke.

"Is he worth it? This Tom. Is he worth everything that you're going through to help him?"

Seb looked out of the window while he thought about the question Geoff had asked him. Was he worth it? No question about it. "Yeah, he is." Seb turned back to Geoff as he answered.

"You like him," Geoff commented as he gave him a small smile.

"I've liked him for a long time. You know I'm bisexual." Seb stopped talking, collecting his thoughts. "Am I happy with what he's had to do to survive? No. I would do anything I could to change that, but I can't. He did what he had to do. It doesn't change how I felt about him then or how I feel about him now. I don't see him as dirty or soiled. I see him as someone who's survived."

Seb stopped talking again, rubbing his forehead. Sitting back in the chair, he stared at Geoff. "He has this inner strength that I don't even think he knows he has. In some strange way, I admire his strength. I know that sounds fucked up, and it probably is. But he had to be strong to do what he's done and not turn to drugs or alcohol. He keeps himself clean and is safe. Always. I don't know if I could have done what he's done to survive. I don't know if I could have survived it. But he has. So what does that say about him?"

Geoff made no comment, but he frowned, leaning back in his chair clearly thinking over what Seb had relayed to him.

Seb stared at him, hoping that he would understand. Finally, he nodded. "Yes, I guess you have to be strong. But I don't know if I could behave towards him the way that you have. You've looked past what he's done, who he's had to be, to see the man he is. You mentioned he lived with this Adam. Are there others?"

"Yeah. I'm not sure of the number, but I think either two or three others around the same age or younger."

"How old is Tom?"

"Nineteen."

"Nineteen? He's been doing this since he was fifteen?" Geoff raised his eyebrows.

"Yeah and he helps the others as well. Didn't want them to make the same mistakes he had."

Geoff leaned forward, resting his forearms on his desk. "Alright. Here's what we're going to do. You are going to find him and see how he is. It must be hard to find a body, let alone a body of someone you know. Plus, he has the others as well. Find him and make sure he's okay. If you need any time off or need someone to help or talk to, come to me."

Seb stared at Geoff, opening and closing his mouth several times. Geoff's acceptance wasn't what he'd expected when he'd began to tell him everything that had happened recently. He didn't know what to say.

Take a Chance

Geoff smiled at him. "Go Seb. Find him, and call me if you need anything?"

"I don't know what to say. Are you sure?" Seb asked.

"Go and call me if you need anything," Geoff told him in a firm voice.

Seb nodded and stood. "Thanks. Really. Thanks."

Geoff nodded. "I hope everything turns out alright for you."

Seb nodded again and left the room. He went to his desk and shut down his computer before he gathered his belongings and left the office. He rushed to his car and, before long, was heading in the direction of where Tom lived, hoping that everything was alright.

When Seb arrived, he drove up and down the street. Unfortunately, there were a number of empty properties, and he didn't know which one would be the one he lived in. There were two options. Either he tried to enter every empty property, or drive to where he knew prostitutes hung out and tried to find one of the guys that lived with Tom. He had only seen two fleetingly that first time he had seen Tom so wasn't too sure what they looked like. He smacked the steering wheel as he swore. His idea wasn't going to plan. He had assumed there would be only one empty property, and he would be able to walk in and find him.

Seb smacked the steering wheel again and looked up at the car roof as he leaned his head back against the headrest. Closing his eyes, he looked forward again as he opened them and caught sight of two teenagers emerging from the back of the houses. One with light hair and the other had dark hair. They looked familiar, and that was enough for him.

He got out of the car, slamming the door shut, and ran over to them. "Hey, do you know Tom?"

They both stared at him blankly before the dark-haired one answered, crossing his arms over his chest, glaring at Seb. "Why? Who are you?"

"I'm his friend Seb. I don't know if he's mentioned me, but I haven't heard from him all week. Can you tell me where he is?"

Seb watched as they looked at each other like they were silently communicating. The blond-haired one nodded to the other and turned to him.

"I'll show you. It can be difficult to get into if you don't know where to look. But I'll warn you now. He won't be able to say much." The blond one told him.

"Why?" Seb asked, stomach dropping. Was Tom ill? Had something happened to him?

"You'll see when you get there. Come on."

Seb followed them as they led him down the alley and showed him the fence so he could enter. He hesitated, not sure what he would find when he walked in and concerned as to how Tom would react. But, eventually, he pushed it aside and started to climb through when one of them reached out to stop him.

"The back door also has a board covering it, but you can pull that back and enter through it. He's been drinking. Adam's death has hit him hard, and he thinks it's his fault. We've told him it's not and that Adam went off on his own, but he's having a hard time believing it." The dark-haired teenager told him.

Seb nodded and thanked them before he continued to climb through. He walked towards the door, suddenly nervous about what he was doing. What if Tom didn't want to know him anymore? What if he blamed him for what had happened to his friend? He'd been spending a lot of time with him recently and might feel like he had abandoned his friends.

Seb rubbed his fingers across his lips and stood outside the door. Should he go in? He paced back and forth as he stared at the door, then he stopped. He was here, and he cared for Tom and wanted to be there for him to lean on.

Pulling the board away from the back door, Seb entered the house and could hear the murmur of people talking. He followed the voices and found himself stood outside the lounge looking in. It was clear that Tom had been drinking. There were empty bottles around him, and he had an unfocused look to him with rosy cheeks. His head bobbed on his shoulders like he was keeping beat to a tune only he could hear.

"Tom."

Tom looked up at him, and his face froze.

"What the fuck are you doing here?"

Chapter Fourteen

Tom stared at Seb. Why was he fucking here? Who did he think he was just turning up like this?

Staggering to his feet, he took several steps forward to steady himself. He'd had a bit to drink. Well, he'd had a lot to drink. After what he'd been through, he felt like he deserved it.

"Come on. I asked you a question. Why are you here?" Tom demanded, swaying.

"Looking for you." Seb stood by the doorway, not quite in the room.

"Well, you've seen me now, so fuck off." He suddenly smirked at him. "Unless you've got some money on ya, then we can have a quick fuck."

Tom smiled to himself. No better way to get rid of Seb then that.

This was Seb's entire fault anyway. If he hadn't been nice and caring, he'd never have spent so much time with him and neglected his mates. And now one of them was dead. It was all his fault. The fucker!

Seb was staring at him with his eyes wide and his lips parted.

"I came to see if you're alright," Seb told him, taking a couple of steps into the room.

Ben turned to him. "I'm outta here," he mumbled before he stood and staggered out of the room using the wall for support.

Tom turned to Seb. "Now look what you've done. Oh well, you can make it worth my while. I've got condoms somewhere," he muttered as he patted his pockets. "How d'you want me? Hmm. Hands and knees? Against the wall? Bent over something?"

Seb raised his hand in front of him. "Stop it. Just shut the fuck up! I didn't come here for that. I'm worried about you. I haven't seen you all week."

"You're worried. Yeah, like you care." Tom snorted.

"I do. Would I be here now if I didn't care about you?"

"We both know why you're here. Blow job or a fuck." Tom smirked to himself. He lowered his hand slowly down his chest, tweaking his nipples until they were hard. Sliding his hand down, Tom grabbed his crotch then undid his button and lowered his zip.

He could see Seb watching him as he pulled his cock out and slowly stroked himself. "What d'you say? I'm up for it, are you?"

Seb suddenly growled and pushed him up against the wall grabbing his top in his fist. "I didn't come here for that. Stop using the fact that I like you against me." Seb pushed away from him and turned away. "When you've sobered up and realise what a dick you've been, come find me and we'll talk."

"Bastard," Tom screamed as Seb stormed from the room. He

stuffed his limp dick back in his jeans, swaying dangerously. He saw the bottle on the floor and staggered over to it. He picked it up and looked at it before throwing it against the wall as he screamed out. He stood there for a minute watching the liquid run down the wall, panting heavily before dropping to the floor and staring at the puddle that was forming on the floor.

Ben walked back into the room and sat next to him before putting an arm over Tom's shoulders. Tom dropped his head onto Ben's chest, squeezing his eyes shut as they burned and itched. He drew in a shaky breath then sobbed into Ben's chest, gripping his top as his body shook.

Next day, Tom woke up, and he knew this was what being dead felt like. His head pounded and his stomach tossed and turned like he was going to throw up at any moment. His mouth felt like it had been possessed by the dead with his tongue glued to the roof of his mouth. He slowly rolled over and tried to sit up, which was a bad thing to do. He felt his stomach lurch and he had seconds to make it to the toilet as bile burned up his throat. He stumbled there as quickly as he could and dropped to his knees, hugging the bowl as he revisited the previous night's drinking session. It tasted far worse coming back up than it had going down.

When he had finished throwing up, Tom sat back and rested his head on the arm he had on the toilet seat. Now he felt worse. He could smell his vomit, and he was pretty sure even the dead would avoid him now.

Tom stood, slowly, and turned on the tap at the sink, seeing a trickle of water come out. Rinsing his mouth out as best he could and trying to ease the burning sensation in his throat, Tom gratefully swallowed the cool liquid. He looked around for something to freshen his mouth with before realising they'd ran out of toothpaste and hadn't bothered to buy any more. He groaned as he leaned his head against the cool cracked tiles on the bathroom wall. The coolness seeped into his hot and sweaty skin, and he gasped as saliva flooded his mouth. He swallowed it down trying not to be sick again.

"How're you feeling?"

Tom turned to see Ben staring at him from the doorway. He tried to smile but wasn't sure if he had pulled it off or not.

"How do I look?"

"Like shit."

"Gee, thanks, mate."

Ben smirked at him. "Want a bacon buttie? I brought some--"

Tom didn't hear the rest of the sentence as he was too busy throwing up again.

"That's a no then." Ben chuckled as he left the room.

Tom flipped him off as he continued to retch.

❋ ❋ ❋

A few hours later found Tom sat outside Seb's house, waiting for him to come home, again. He felt like shit. The things he'd said to him, the things he'd done. His stomach turned at the thought of what he'd done in front of Seb. He didn't think he could be sick again. He was pretty sure there was nothing left in his stomach to bring up as he had done such a thorough job of it earlier. He groaned thinking about what he'd done. For fuck's sake, he had got his dick out and started jerking himself, and in front of Seb. Like the whore he was.

Looking up at the darkening sky, Tom questioned why he'd come here. Seb probably didn't want anything to do with him now, and how could he blame him? Seb had gone to his house yesterday looking for him because he was worried, and he'd turned it against him. He knew deep down it wasn't Seb's fault. He could see how Adam's behaviour was becoming erratic, more dangerous. Ben had tried everything he could to help him, but Adam hadn't wanted it.

Poor Ben. His head was screwed up over Adam's death. Tom had spent most of the week trying to convince him that it wasn't his fault that Adam was dead. Ben had done everything he could have to help Adam out, to try and convince him to take someone with him when he went out. But Adam had been self-destructive, and it had ultimately resulted in his murder. Tom was grateful that they had made up. He didn't want to lose Ben as a friend. He didn't have that many.

When Tom heard a car approaching, he looked up and eventually watched it turn onto the drive. He stood as the car stopped and watched as Seb turned the engine off. Even from where he stood, he could see the clenched jaw and white knuckles gripping the steering wheel. Seb looked furious as he stared at him, and Tom swallowed as he pushed his hands into his jeans pockets.

Seb sat for such a long time in the car that Tom thought he wasn't going to get out before the door opened and Seb stood. He ignored him as he unloaded bags of groceries from the boot and walked past him to the door, only stopping to open it before walking inside.

Tom stood staring out at the street, waiting to hear the door slam shut behind him but heard nothing. He turned to look at the door, seeing that it stood open. Taking that as an invitation, he walked over to it and went into the house, closing the door behind him. He walked towards the kitchen and watched as Seb put the groceries away.

"Have you had a shower? Food?" Seb asked him, not turning to look at him.

"No." Tom shook his head.

"Go upstairs, shower and put some clean clothes on. I'll cook something."

Tom stared at him before he walked out of the room. He stopped when he realised that Seb hadn't looked at him once since he had entered the house. He cringed at the thought; he didn't want Seb to be angry with him even though he knew he deserved it. He grabbed the handrail as he slowly walked upstairs.

Chapter Fifteen

Tom came downstairs feeling relatively human again. It was amazing how much of a difference having a shower and putting clean clothes on could make you feel. He'd also been able to brush his teeth and finally his mouth felt like it was clean and fresh.

Walking into the kitchen expecting to see Seb there, Tom was surprised to find it empty. Going into the lounge, Tom found Seb sat watching TV and drinking a bottle of beer. He waited and watched Seb, but it appeared as if Seb was ignoring him. He sighed and ran his hand through his hair. He didn't know what to say to make things better between them.

"Food won't be long. Lasagne," Seb told him eventually, not glancing in his direction.

Tom cleared his throat before responding. "Yeah. Thanks."

Sitting next to Seb on the sofa, Tom looked at him. It appeared like

Seb was ignoring him, but that couldn't be right because he'd let him clean up and had cooked a meal for him. It was time he manned up and did the right thing.

"I'm sorry, Seb. What I did and said yesterday was out of order. I was drunk, and you had come to check up on me, and I treated you like shit."

Seb didn't say anything. He just sat watching TV. Tom stared at him waiting for him to respond, but the longer he waited, the worse the butterflies in his stomach became. He couldn't sit still and fidgeted on the seat, crossing his legs then uncrossing them, leaning forward before sitting back. He couldn't stand the silence from Seb.

Eventually Tom leaned forward, twisting on the sofa to face Seb. "Please say something. I know I was out of line. Tell me what I have to say or do to make things better."

Seb finally turned his head to look at him. Oh, he was pissed. He could see it in the hard stare and clenched jaw.

"Do you know what I've been through this week?" Not waiting for an answer, Seb continued, "Wait, no, you don't because you disappeared off the face of the fucking planet. I've had to deal with the police. In work! I had to tell my boss everything! And guess what was worse? Not knowing how you were, how you were doing. Not knowing if you were alive or if you had gone back to selling yourself. I haven't slept. I've barely eaten because I couldn't find you. I didn't even know where you fucking lived!" Seb was shouting now as he looked at Tom and leaned forward towards him. "I was fucking scared, Tom! Scared that you would do something stupid, and I wouldn't be there to help you."

Toms own anger suddenly erupted, and he lashed out, "Help me? I don't need anybody's help. I've managed on my own for years."

"What? You've managed? By being a rent boy? Do you call that managing because I fucking don't." Seb stared at him then shook his head. Standing, Seb walked over to the window, staring out. He crossed his arms over his chest. Silence descended in the room, interrupted by the sound of the TV.

"I did what I had to do to survive. I had nothing. Nothing, Seb. What else could I do?"

The anger appeared to leave Seb, his shoulders slumping. Seb ran a hand through his hair. He sighed before looking back at Tom. "I know. I just wanted to help you, be there for you. What is so wrong with that? What is so wrong with having someone want to help you?"

"Who would want to help me? I'm a whore! No one wants to help a whore." Tom swallowed, glancing away. "Who could even love me? Nobody. Just look at my parents, they kicked me out. The people I was supposed to trust above everyone else kicked me out and left me on the fuckin' streets. I thought they loved me, that they would accept me, but I was wrong. They didn't give a shit about how I was goin' to look after myself." Tom glanced back up at Seb. "I've whored myself so I could eat, Seb. I'm nothing, nothing but used goods. So tell me, Seb, who would want to help me?" Tom stared at Seb before he dropped his head in his hands. His chest heaved and his throat burned, and he swallowed against the emotions trying to overwhelm him.

"I would," Seb whispered to him. "I do."

Tom shook his head, not bothering to look up. God, he wanted to believe Seb. But what if he was lying? He wanted to trust him. Wanted to believe in Seb. But didn't he already? Isn't that why he'd come here?

"I thought you knew that. I thought last weekend would've made you see that. I don't know what to say to you to make you understand how I feel. I've told you that what you've had to do to survive doesn't affect how I feel. I don't see you that way. I see you, Tom."

"I just don't get it. I'm a whore. I'm used goods," Tom muttered in a small voice.

Seb stood and walked over to him before squatting in front of him. "I've said it before, and I'll say it again. You did what you had to do to survive. It doesn't change how I feel about you."

Tom closed his eyes when they started to burn and he took a shuddering breath as he tried to stop the tears from falling, but he couldn't stop them from spilling over. He tried to breathe, but it ended up a sob. He felt arms reach around him and hold him tight and he finally, finally let go and poured out all the misery and grief he'd been feeling for years. He grabbed Seb's top and held on tight as harsh sobs racked his body. Seb held him tightly, rubbing his back, letting him cry.

He wasn't sure how long he sat crying, but his throat burned when he finally stopped. It felt like all he had done recently was cry, but for some reason, he finally felt free, like the tears had cleansed him. His chest felt lighter, and he sniffed as he blinked his eyes to clear the remaining tears still gathered there. He looked up at Seb before asking him quietly, "Why? Why me?"

"I see you. I've always seen you." He smiled at him as he wiped the tears from his face. "Even though you weren't around, I thought of you. I would wonder how you were or what you were doing."

"I just can't believe it. I know you've told me before, but I just seem to have problems trusting it, you know."

Seb nodded. "Yeah. I understand. I can't imagine how difficult things have been for you, but I'm here now and I'm not going anywhere. I'm willing to face the parents for you. I'm that serious about us. But I guess the question is, do you want me too? Because I don't want to be in this on my own. I lost you once, and I don't want to lose you again."

Tom stared at him. Could he believe him? Should he believe him?

Yes on both.

He leaned forward and gently kissed Seb on the lips. He leaned back and looked at Seb before kissing him again. He felt Seb respond to him, licking his bottom lip before gently sucking it into his mouth.

Tom groaned as he opened his mouth and sucked on Seb's tongue. He reached his hand up and held the back of Seb's neck. They tangled tongues, slowly at first, tasting each other. They'd kissed before, but this felt like more. More emotion, more of a connection. Maybe it was because Tom was finally letting go. The intensity, the deep connection that was building between them, stole his breath away, and he gripped Seb tightly.

Tom leaned back, breaking the kiss to pull Seb's shirt of over his head. He moved forward and kissed Seb, taking his time to explore every inch of Seb's mouth. Tom ended the kiss and moved to nuzzle Seb's jaw, feeling his stubble on his lips. Tom moved further down, biting Seb's' neck, eliciting a moan from Seb and feeling him shiver. Tom loved the sounds Seb made. He loved being the cause of them, knowing he could make Seb tremble beneath him.

Biting Seb's collar bone, Tom soothed the sting by running his tongue across it, licking slowly, tasting him. Seb's breath hitched and Tom smiled against Seb's skin. Tom continued to lick and kiss his way down Seb's chest until he reached his nipples. He licked across one then blew on it, watching it harden. Seb trembled, causing Tom to glance up at him.

Seb was watching everything he did, his eyes wide, lips parted and skin flushed.

Tom licked the same nipple again then slowly sucked it into his mouth, flicking the nub with his tongue. Seb groaned, grabbing Tom's hair and pushing Tom's face into his chest. Sucking and flicking the nub, Tom felt Seb's body move beneath him. Tom's fingers plucked Seb's other nipple, feeling that one harden too. He moved his mouth over to the other nipple and sucked that one in, again flicking it with his tongue.

"Oh fuck, Tom," Seb groaned out, hand tightening its grip in Tom's hair.

Tom moved between Seb's nipples, licking and sucking them. Biting one gently, he felt Seb jerk, gasping loudly.

Seb pulled Tom's head away and kissed him again, forcefully, deepening the kiss as their tongues duelled. Seb moved to straddle him and pulled Tom's shirt off over his head before leaning forward to kiss him again.

When Tom started to undo his belt, Seb stopped him. "Are you sure?"

Tom looked at him and could see how much Seb wanted him. The lust was evident in his face, his cheeks flushed, lips parted. "Yeah, I am."

Seb stood and walked away for a minute before coming back. He stood in front of Tom and held his hand out. Tom put his hand in Seb's and allowed him to pull him off the sofa, then lead him out of the living room and up the stairs. When they reached Seb's bedroom and went inside, Seb turned and faced him. "Are you sure?" he asked again.

Tom stepped forward and held Seb's head between his hands, kissing him, letting the action answer for him. Seb trailed his hands over Tom's bare chest before tweaking his nipples. Tom moaned and leaned into the touch, watching Seb's hands on his body. Seb dropped down and sucked one Tom's nipples into his mouth, rolling it with his tongue before flicking it.

"Oh, God..."

Seb smiled against his skin before moving to Tom's other nipple, licking it, then moving down Tom's chest and abdomen, kissing and gently biting as he went.

Tom ran his fingers through Seb's hair and held him as he watched. Seb popped open the button on Tom's jeans and slid the zipper down. He pushed his jeans down over Tom's hips, causing Tom's cock to bounce on his abdomen, leaving some precome there.

Seb trailed a finger up the underside of Tom's cock and gently rubbed the bundle of nerves under the head. Tom closed his eyes and moaned in pleasure. He opened his eyes when he felt Seb's hand encase his cock and stroke it slowly but firmly. He watched as Seb looked up at him and, not breaking eye contact, lean forward licking his way from the base to the crown before he took the entire length into his mouth and throat.

"Oh fuck....." Tom groaned as he stared down at Seb. His hips bucked and his hands grabbed the sides of Seb's face. He tried not to move his hips, but he seemed to have lost all control. He watched as Seb bobbed up and down, twirling his tongue around the head before swallowing him again.

Letting go of Tom's dick, Seb stood up and pulled Tom towards the bed where he pushed him down and finished removing Tom's clothes. Seb then hurriedly stripped out of his own until he stood naked in front of Tom.

Tom stared up at Seb. He knew Seb went to the gym, and he had seen him virtually naked before, but fuck, he looked hot. He could see how ripped he was, but what caught his eye was Seb's dick. Long and thick and so hard, the head wet as precome bubbled from the slit.

Before he could stop himself, Tom leaned forward and sucked the head into his mouth before pulling off and swirling his tongue around it. He licked it from head to base and back up again before taking him down whole and swallowing around the head. At least he'd had plenty of practice doing this, and he wanted to give Seb the best blow job he'd ever had. He hollowed his cheeks and sucked tightly as he slowly moved off him, only to repeat the movement. He could feel Seb's hips moving, and he grabbed hold of them to stop the movement.

He looked up to find Seb staring down at him, his mouth hanging open. He felt Seb's hand caress his cheek before gently pushing him away.

"As much as I want you to finish that, I'd rather have you fuck me."

"You want me to fuck you?" Tom asked as his eyes flickered over Seb's face. He'd never fucked anyone before. In all the time he'd been hooking, he'd never been asked to fuck someone. He'd always been the one on the receiving end.

Seb nodded. "Yeah, I do."

Tom blinked, not knowing what to say. He never imagined that Seb would let him top, but watched as he reached into a drawer and pulled out a condom and lube. Seb lay on the bed and pulled Tom over him, pulling him down so they could kiss again.

Lying on top of Seb, Tom loved the feeling of Seb's hard body under him. He kissed him, feeling their tongues move together before Tom started kissing his way down Seb's jaw and neck. He sucked a mark on Seb's neck, loving the way Seb's body twitched and listening to him moan in pleasure. Staring at the mark he left, Tom smiled. Everyone would know what Seb had been up to.

Continuing down Seb's body, Tom stopped at his nipples, sucking the left one into his mouth, gently biting it before licking it. Seb's hands gripped his hair again, holding him.

"Sensitive?" Tom asked, feeling Seb's body shiver as he flicked his nipple.

"Yeah," Seb gasped out as Tom's tongue circled his nipple.

Tom moved over to the other nipple and gave it the same

treatment, smiling when Seb shuddered. A few more flicks of his tongue, then Tom moved down Seb's chest and abdomen, kissing and biting, leaving marks on Seb's skin.

Straddling Seb's hips, Tom's fingers traced Seb's body, the first time he'd had the opportunity to really look at one. The valleys and dips. What made Seb shiver or made him laugh. The way Seb's breath would catch, his body shudder, his skin erupt in goose bumps.

Eventually Tom reached Seb's hard, leaking cock. He held it up and looked at it, watching the precome leak from the slit and a string form as it dropped onto his abdomen, keeping it connected to his cock. Stroking it slowly, Tom watched the skin cover the head then pull down revealing his slit. Seb was uncut and Tom wanted to run his tongue over and under the skin, suck up his juices.

Moving his hands down Seb's legs, Tom leaned forward, running his tongue over the head then sucking it into his mouth while moving his tongue around, tasting him. Pulling the foreskin back, Tom ran his tongue under it, licking up more of Seb's juices, moaning at his taste.

Stroking Seb, Tom continued to lick and suck on the head, enjoying the sounds Seb made. Moving down, Tom traced the large vein running down Seb's cock with his tongue, sucking the skin at the base into his mouth.

Licking back up, Tom took the head back into his mouth and sucked as he bobbed. Reaching blindly, Tom found the lube and condom Seb had left.

Opening the lube, Tom poured some on his fingers, rubbing them together. He circled Seb's hole, feeling the muscle twitch. As he pushed a finger in, Tom swallowed Seb's shaft. Seb was smooth, hot and tight around his finger and Tom could hardly wait to feel it on his dick.

"Oh fuck, Tom!"

Take a Chance

Tom hummed, the vibrations moving up Seb's shaft, and his hips jerked. Tom continued to move his finger slowly in and out of Seb's hole until he was sure Seb was loose enough for a second finger. He then pushed a second one in as well, twisting them until he hit Seb's prostate, hearing Seb moan in pleasure, hips bucking in response.

Seb cried out again as he pushed a third finger in and started moving them, scissoring them to help the muscle loosen up more. When he felt Seb was nice and loose, he removed his fingers and reached over for the condom, opening the packet and rolling it down his dick. Adding lube, Tom stroked himself to make sure he was covered.

Spreading Seb's legs, Tom lay between them, lifting Seb's legs up over his arms. He looked into Seb's eyes as he reached around and lined up his cock with Seb's hole, rubbing slowly over it, watching Seb. Seb bit his lip and nodded to Tom and Tom slowly pushed in.

Tom felt resistance at first that suddenly gave way. Once he'd breached the muscle, he stopped, trying to gain some control, panting hard and waiting for Seb to adjust. Seb was so tight around his cock. He was also hot and smooth. Tom squeezed his eyes shut as he tried not to come, moaning as he tried to keep control, gripping Seb's thighs. He didn't want to come too soon. He wanted to savour this moment.

Tom held on, his body trembling, sweat breaking out and covering his skin as he waited for Seb to tell him it was alright to continue. Tom didn't want to hurt him. He knew how painful it was to have someone fuck you when you weren't ready, and they weren't patient enough to wait while you got used to it.

Seb nodded to him when he was ready, and Tom pushed in, not stopping until he was in fully. Tom dropped down onto Seb, kissing him, gripping Seb's shoulders with his hands.

Tom moved in and out of Seb, groaning at how tight Seb was

around his dick. Seb wrapped his legs around Tom's hips, moving his hips up and down in time with Tom's thrusts in and out of his body. Tom reached up until he found Seb's hands and entwined their fingers together as he looked down at him.

Seb's hazel eyes were staring straight up at him with a look that Tom could only describe as adoration. Tom understood that feeling. He felt the same way about Seb even with the trust issues he had. It was as if he could feel the emotions coming from Seb, and he responded to them.

Tom wanted to take it slow and easy and enjoy being with Seb this way, but his body had other ideas. Feeling Seb's body wrapped around his, squeezing him tight, spurred his own body on and he moved faster and harder in and out of Seb's arse.

Within minutes, he was grunting as he hammered into Seb, Seb moaning. He reached down between them and grabbed Seb's cock, stroking him as he continued to thrust harder into Seb. He wanted Seb to come before him. Wanted to know that he'd made him come.

When Seb tensed up around him, Tom knew he was close. Seb arched up, head slamming back into the pillow, crying out.

Tom felt Seb's hole tighten around his dick, warmth spreading between their bodies. Sweat dripped from Tom's forehead, his body shaking, his balls tightening. Tingling spread from them and up his shaft and through his arse. Tom groaned, ropes of come shooting from his dick, his body jerking and shaking.

When he'd finished coming, Tom slumped on top of Seb, panting. Seb wrapped his arms around him and Tom turned his head so he could nuzzle Seb's neck.

"Wow," Seb gasped out.

"Yeah," Tom agreed. That had been the most intense orgasm of his life.

Take a Chance

Lifting his head, Tom glanced down at Seb, taking in his features, then leaned down, kissing him gently. Seb moved into the kiss, and they stayed like that for a couple of minutes, sharing languid kisses, gently touching each other.

Eventually, Tom pulled away and, holding the end of the condom, pulled out of Seb. He removed the condom and tied it off before disposing of it in the bin next to the bed. He got up and walked to the bathroom to get a wet cloth for Seb, and then came back and wiped his stomach and chest down.

"Thanks." Seb smiled up at him as he watched Tom.

Tom stood and waited. Now they'd had sex what would Seb do? What would happen now? At this point, he usually got away as quickly as possible, but this wasn't one of those times. Seb wasn't someone paying him for sex. He'd never been with someone under these circumstances, and he felt out of place because of it.

As if he sensed his inner turmoil, Seb stood and hugged him. "Let's get dressed and have something to eat. It shouldn't take long to heat the food up again."

Tom nodded and picked up his jeans off the floor before getting dressed. Seb only had his jeans on when he turned and reached out for Tom's hand. Pulling Tom behind him, Seb went downstairs. In the living room, Seb picked up their T-shirts from the floor and passed Tom's to him.

Following Seb, Tom pulled his own and watched Seb check the lasagne in the oven. "Still good," Seb said. "Grab us a couple of plates, will you? Oh, and a couple of beers from the fridge."

Tom grabbed the items as Seb put some veg bags into the microwave and turned it on. It didn't take long to plate everything up, and soon they were in the living room eating.

After they'd finished, Seb stood and reached for his hand, pulling him up from the sofa. He didn't say a word as he led him upstairs back to his bedroom. Tom stood and watched as Seb stripped off and smiled at him. He walked over to him and pulled his shirt off before undoing his jeans and pulling them down. Tom stepped out of them and let Seb lead him to bed. Was Seb going to want to fuck him now? Seb pushed him onto the bed before he settled himself between his legs. Tom was already hard, precome leaking. Seb looked down his body, and then grabbed his cock and stared straight into his eyes as he swallowed him down. Tom's hips bucked, and he tried to stop them moving, but it was hard.

"Don't stop moving. I want you to fuck my face." Seb groaned before sucking the head back in.

Tom stared down at him. Did he just say that? He felt Seb's hands push his hips and move them up and down. Oh yeah, he definitely wanted Tom to fuck his face.

Tom reached down and held Seb's face as he started to do what Seb wanted. God, it felt so good, and he groaned as he watched his cock move in and out of Seb's mouth. He was thrusting hard and didn't stop until he was all the way in, but Seb didn't seem to mind. If anything, he was enjoying it just as much as Tom, moaning around his dick.

Tom had lost all sense of time when he felt a wet finger circle his hole and slowly push in. He groaned at the dual sensations. It felt too much, but at the same time, not quite enough.

Seb pulled off his dick and pushed Tom's legs back to his chest before dropping back down. Next thing Tom felt was Seb's tongue as it circled the finger in his hole.

Tom shouted out. No one had ever done this to him before and it felt fucking amazing. Seb licked and sucked at Tom's hole before removing his finger, pushing his tongue in and fucking him with it.

Tom was moaning and blabbering incoherently. He wasn't making much sense. He couldn't stop his hips moving, and he was vaguely aware of pushing his arse into Seb's face, begging for more. Tom never knew having his arse eaten would feel this good.

In and out. In and out. Sweat broke out over Tom's skin as intense pleasure flowed through him. When Seb's tongue pulled out and licked his hole, Tom jerked. It was almost too much for him to take. The pleasure was overwhelming.

When two fingers breached him, Tom cried out. Then suddenly Seb touched something inside him and he cried out again, shooting all over his chest and stomach as his orgasm caught him by surprise. Tom jerked until he finished coming and opened his eyes to see Seb leaning over him, licking him clean. He then kissed his way up his chest and neck. He hadn't been aware that Seb had even moved.

"Enjoy that?" Seb murmured from where he was kissing Tom's skin.

"Huh?"

Seb chuckled before he looked up. Tom could see the smile on his face and reached a hand up to caress his cheek. Seb leaned into it and closed his eyes. Tom stared at him, amazed that Seb showed these emotions so openly in front of him. He'd never experienced any of that when growing up. His parents' faces had rarely expressed emotions, well, unless he'd done something wrong. They had rarely hugged him or told him that he was loved and yet here was Seb, being so open with his emotions.

"Hope you have a quick recovery time because I'm gonna ride you next."

Tom inhaled shakily before he nodded. Yeah, this was definitely a night of firsts.

Chapter Sixteen

Seb woke up the next morning and stretched then winced. His arse was sore. He smiled to himself when he remembered why. Tom had fucked him twice more that night, and Seb had enjoyed every minute of it.

Rolling over, Seb watched Tom sleep. It was only during sex and sleep that Tom lost the haunted, guarded look that he always wore. A look Seb detested.

Lifting his hand, Seb reached over and stroked the hair from Tom's face, rubbing the strands between his fingers. He wanted Tom to stay here with him, but knew that might not happen. Given the way things had been for Tom, it would take some time for him to believe that Seb wanted him to live with him. He sighed to himself as he tried to think of a way he could help Tom out. He knew Tom wouldn't leave his friends, and he admired that about him. He was loyal, and even though he had a way out of the life he'd been forced to live, he still thought about the others, cared about them.

The house had three bedrooms, so Seb had two spare, but there were three others, and they couldn't all stay unless they shared. There was also the money. He couldn't afford to help look after three other people, and knowing Tom, he wouldn't expect things for free either.

Trying to find a solution, Seb laid watching Tom sleep, but not finding one, he quietly got out of bed and went for a shower. Walking slowly, as he could feel his arse twinge, he grabbed some clothes and closed the bathroom door behind him. When he finished, he went downstairs and made coffee and breakfast and decided to watch some TV, letting Tom sleep in.

It was about an hour later when Seb heard the floorboards creak above him and knew Tom was up. He heard the shower come on and got up to make him some breakfast. By the time Tom came down, Seb had the breakfast ready and some fresh coffee made. He turned to him as he entered the kitchen. "Morning. Breakfast and coffee?"

"Yes, please."

Seb watched as Tom seemed to struggle to look him in the eye. He'd been like that last night after the first time they'd slept together. A little shy and unsure of himself. He found it sweet. He walked over to him and kissed him on the lips. "Come on, have your breakfast and we'll decide what we're doing for the rest of the day. Although a trip to the police station is necessary."

"Why? I told them everything I know." Tom exclaimed as he followed Seb into the lounge and sat on the sofa.

"I know, but I guess they just want to try and get as much information as they can. I don't know what they found, so even if we think it means nothing, it might be important to them. We can't let what happened to Adam happen to someone else."

Tom sighed and leaned back on the sofa, closing his eyes. "I know.

It's just all I see is him lying there, and I just want to try and forget about it. That isn't how I want to remember him. He was a good friend, and he looked out for all of us."

"How's everyone else taking it?" Seb asked him.

Tom sighed again and leaned forward resting his forearms on his thighs. "Ben's in a bad way. They hung out together all the time. They really were best friends. He feels so guilty that he wasn't there for him."

"I thought Adam had gone out on his own?"

Tom nodded as he ate a mouthful of toast and swallowed it before answering. "Yeah, he did. Ben tried to convince him not to, but after the attack, he just changed. It was like he didn't want to look out for himself."

"Maybe he was proving to himself that he could take care of himself, that the attack hadn't affected him." Seb shrugged. "I can't say. I never knew him."

Tom was silent for a few seconds, then nodded. "I think you're right. It does seem to fit how he'd been behaving. Careless, risky. I'll miss him though, that's for sure. He was a good laugh. No matter what shit we dealt with, he always found joy in something. He'd seen a lot of shit on the streets, knew about the pitfalls too. Seen some of his street friends die taking drugs."

"What about the other two? Luke and Matt, didn't you say?" Seb asked, curious about them.

"Yeah. I don't know. I want to keep them safe."

Seb sighed and looked at the floor. How could he say what was on his mind? Should he just come out with it? He didn't want to frighten Tom away, but he didn't want him to leave either.

"I want you to stay."

Take a Chance

"I can tonight, but then I'll have to head back."

"No." Taking a deep breath, he tried again. "I want you to move in here with me."

Tom stared at him, mouth opening and closing several times, but no words came out. Shit, that wasn't what he wanted. Seb could see Tom tensing up, so interrupted before he could say anything on his offer. "I know you have your reasons for saying no. You need to look out for the others, it's too soon, you're a rent boy, etc. I know what I'm asking here. I looked for you, Tom. Scared out of my mind for you. I don't want to go through that again. And to be honest, I don't want you going back to selling yourself, not if we're going to have any form of a relationship. I can help you finish your education if you want, or find a job. Just, please think about what I'm asking here." Seb all but begged him.

"What about the others? I can't leave them," Tom told him, shaking his head.

"I know. I'm trying to think of some way to help them, but I don't know right now. I thought about them sharing the other bedrooms, but it's space and money, and I can't afford to look after them too. I might talk to my boss at work, Geoff. He's a good guy, and I'm pretty sure he'll know someone who could help us. Will you think about it?"

Seb watched Tom, the struggle showing clearly on his face. Every emotion was broadcast for Seb to see. Seb didn't know what more he could say to convince Tom to give it a try. Considering he was a solicitor, he was piss poor with his words today.

They sat in silence until Tom whispered, "I want to. You've no idea how much I want to."

"Then what is it?" Seb asked him. If he wanted to give it a try, why wasn't he?

"What happens to me when one day you wake up and realise

you've been wasting your fuckin' life on a whore? We're in such different places right now. I just keep expecting to open my eyes and all this disappears."

"You're afraid I won't want you." It wasn't a question but a statement. Seb understood the reasons why Tom struggled to trust him, but now he could see the fear. Tom was afraid to believe that someone would want him with the past he had. Seb was sure he'd told him that his past didn't matter, but maybe Tom needed to hear it again.

"You know your past means nothing to me, don't you? As I've said, I don't like the fact that you had to do it, but you did, and you survived. Most people who live on the streets become drug users or alcoholics, right?" Tom nodded, so Seb continued, "You haven't become either. You've kept clean and smart. You have a strength to you which I don't even think you know you have. Only someone who is strong could live the way you have and still be here as you are today. I admire that." Seb paused as he thought about what he was going to say next. "Are things going to be all sunshine and rainbows and shit between us? No, I'm sure we'll have days where we argue and want to scream at each other. That's normal in relationships, but I want to do that with you."

"It's just--"

"What?" Seb interrupted him.

Tom shook his head and looked down at the floor. Seb stood up and dropped to his knees in front of him. He reached out and pushed Tom's head back up so they could look at each other. "Move in. We'll figure the rest out as we go."

Kneeling in front of Tom, Seb held Tom's head up, searching his face for what seemed like hours, but eventually he felt more than saw Tom nod. He exhaled, shoulders slumping, smiling at Tom.

"So, today is Sunday, right?" Tom asked him.

"Yeah, why?"

"Don't you go your parents on a Sunday?"

Seb stared at Tom blankly before realising what he had said. "Shit! I completely forgot!"

"Well, you can go to your parents, and I can wait here, then after, we can get my things. How's that?"

"Don't you want to come?" Seb asked him before he smiled. "Can you imagine their faces?"

Tom chuckled with him before shaking his head with a small smile on his face. "Yeah, somehow I don't think they'd let me in, do you?"

Seb shook his head, "No. No, they wouldn't." He frowned as he looked at Tom. "I want you to come soon. I'm not going to hide you."

"Maybe one day, but you kinda have your hands full with my shit. Why add more?"

"Your shit? Nothing we can't work through, right?"

Tom nodded and smiled. "Yeah."

Seb stood up and stretched. "We also need to get you tested."

Tom stood and ran his hands through his hair as he paced in front of Seb. "Shit. I knew we shouldn't have--"

Seb stepped in front of him and put his hands on his shoulders, stopping him. "I wanted to. You've always been safe, haven't you?"

Tom nodded. "And I've been tested a few times too. I was terrified I'd catch something."

"So there's no problem. It's just to make sure." Tom nodded, and Seb kissed him. "Guess I'll get ready and head over. Don't want to though."

Seb stuck his bottom lip out as he pouted at Tom. Tom chuckled and wrapped his arms around him.

"I'll be here when you get back. I'll make it all better."

Seb grinned. "Promise?"

Tom smiled pushing him back. "Go. The sooner you get there, the sooner you come back."

Seb leaned forward and kissed him slowly but thoroughly before leaving the room and jogging upstairs. He wasn't surprised he'd forgotten. The last few days had been hard to get through, and he just wanted to stay home curled up with Tom on the sofa.

Looking down at what he was wearing, Seb realised he needed to change. Knowing his mum, she wouldn't be impressed with his scruffy ripped up jeans, so they had to go. As he changed, he wondered how he was going to tell his parents about him and Tom. First, they would be unhappy that Tom was back in his life considering how they felt about him being gay, and second, they would furious when they knew he was in a relationship with Tom.

Unhappy and furious.

Two words that didn't come close to how his parents would react.

Would they blame Tom for 'making him gay'? Would they listen to him when he told them he'd had other boyfriends? Fuck, this was messed up. He knew his parents were in the wrong with their behaviour and attitude towards gay people, but how would they act towards him when they realised that he liked men also? Would they cut him out of their lives?

Seb knew some people would say he was better off without them if that was how they would be, but they were his parents, and he loved them. Maybe he was stupid but he hoped they would accept him no matter what, but he knew they probably wouldn't.

Was his relationship with Tom worth losing his parents? And what about Josh? Not that they were close now, but how would he react when he found out? Would he turn his back on him as well? Seb sat on his bed thinking through all the implications him being with Tom would bring and the changes that would occur in his life. He had absolutely no regrets in asking him to move in. Yeah, it was soon, but it felt right. And even if things didn't work out between them, he felt better knowing he had helped him, had gotten him off the streets and starting a better life. He'd wanted Tom for a long time, years actually, and he couldn't let him walk out of his life now he was back in it again. He would do anything he could to keep Tom, even potentially lose his family. And with that thought, he realised that he loved Tom. Probably had loved him for some time now. With his mind made up, he finished getting ready.

Megs Pritchard

Chapter Seventeen

As Tom waited at Seb's, wait, no, *their* house-- that was going to take some getting used to-- he cleaned up and had a bit of a nosy. Not that he felt Seb had anything to hide, but he just wanted to be able to look around the place that was now his home. After snooping for a while and finding very little, other than a certain toy collection which would be put to use, he sat down with a coffee and watched some TV. Typical Sunday TV was as crap as he remembered it, especially this close to Christmas, but he wanted to do something to take his mind off the fact that Seb was at his parents. Tom knew Seb wasn't going to say anything about them just yet, and he understood the reasons why. He was pretty sure they would freak out when Seb told them about him, and he didn't want to be around when that happened. However, as his boyfriend--wow, that sounded strange--he would need to be there to offer support, and wasn't that all grown up? Chuckling to himself, he got up to make some more coffee when he heard a car pull into the drive.

Taking a look out of the window, he could see that Seb was back already. Looking at the clock, he was surprised to see that he had only been gone a couple of hours. He hadn't been expecting him back for a while yet. He walked into the kitchen to make a drink for Seb, hearing the front door slam shut and turned when he walked in behind him looking pissed off.

"Everything alright?" he asked him, knowing that the answer was going to be no.

Seb threw his car keys on the side before answering. "No. Josh was there."

"Oh. How's he doing?"

Seb leaned back against the counter as he looked at him. "Like the little shit he is. He wants to leave Uni, get a job, and the parents are okay with it. I don't get it! They weren't happy with him for messing around, and now they just accept him leaving!" Seb opened a drawer and slammed it shut, frustrated with what was happening. Tom didn't understand what the problem was. If Josh wanted to leave, and Uni wasn't for him, why continue doing something that made you unhappy?

"Doesn't he like his course?" Tom asked.

"The course has nothing to do with it. He's bored. He wants to travel the world on some fucking cruise liner! My parents were like, 'okay, Josh, whatever you want Josh.' If I pulled any of the shit Josh has, I'd have been out. He can fuck around with his life and Mum and Dad will be there to pick up the pieces. I ended up storming out." Tom watched as Seb took a deep breath and managed to rein in his anger. "Come on, aren't we supposed to be going somewhere?" Seb smiled at Tom as he walked over and pulled him into his arms. Tom smiled back at him before leaning up to kiss him.

"Yeah, as long as you're still sure."

Seb rolled his eyes before kissing him back. "Yep. This is gonna be the best part of my day. Let's go."

As Tom let Seb pull him out of the kitchen and towards the front door, a car pulled up onto the drive and parked behind Seb's. Tom watched as Seb pulled back the curtain to look out before swearing.

"Fuck! What does he want?"

"Who is it?" Tom asked.

Seb turned around and looked at him. "Josh."

Tom stood still, staring at Seb. Why had Josh come here? He didn't want to see or speak to him just yet. He was nowhere near ready to have any form of conversation with Josh. And did Seb want Josh to know about Tom? Because he knew that would get back to Seb's parents, and they were trying to avoid that.

"Er, what d'you want me to do? Should I go upstairs out of the way?"

The doorbell rang as he waited for Seb to reply. He heard him sigh, then was surprised to see him shake his head. "No. I'd like you to stay here, but it's up to you."

"If he sees me, you know he'll tell your parents."

The doorbell went again followed by the banging on the door. Tom heard a muffled voice. "I know you're here, Seb. Open the door."

Seb stood watching Tom, so Tom made the decision for him. Taking a deep breath, Tom walked to the front door and pulled it open. "Hi, Josh. How're ya doing?" Tom asked, plastering a fake smile on his face.

Josh stared at him with his mouth open before he snarled, "What the fuck are you doing here?"

Take a Chance

Pushing past Tom, Josh stormed up to Seb before turning to point back at Tom. "What the fuck is he doing here?"

"Because I asked him. My house, my choice," Seb stated calmly.

"What? You know how Mum and Dad feel about him. Why would you invite him here?"

"What, that he's gay? I've no problems with that, and you've been to Uni, so you shouldn't have a problem with it either."

Tom watched as Josh opened his mouth and then closed it. He obviously didn't know that Seb knew the truth about him.

"What? You didn't think I knew, did you? You and the parents were quite happy to let me carry on believing that story." Seb shook his head and then stared intently at Josh. "It was you, wasn't it? You got her pregnant."

Tom shook his head as he stared at the floor. Of course, it was Josh's. He turned away from them as he ran his hands through his hair. He turned back to face Josh, the fucker! Everything he had been through had been because of Josh and the fact that Josh wouldn't accept responsibility for his actions.

"You knew all along that you were the father. All along! I ended up homeless because of you, living on the fuckin' streets. You could have said anything, at any time, to help me, but you stood there and said nothing. Nothing!" Tom screamed the last word at Josh.

Josh looked away, staring at his feet, not saying a word.

"Why didn't you fuckin' say anything, Josh? We were best mates, and when I needed you the most, you weren't there for me."

"You have no idea what it was like at home--"

"I do, so don't use that excuse," Seb interrupted. "Mum and Dad would have stood by you like they have done through all the shit you've caused. It doesn't matter what you say or do. They stand by you. Yeah, you could have said something, so why didn't you?"

Josh stood, staring defiantly at Seb, neither one of them backing down.

"It was easier for you to let them think it was me, wasn't it. Then you didn't have to own up, didn't have to face your fuckin' responsibilities. You piece of shit. How many other people have taken the fuckin' blame for something you've done? All that stuff we did, you never got the blame for any of that shit, so how did you get away with it all? Someone else take the fall for you? Did you stand by and watch them be blamed and say nothing?" Tom demanded.

Josh suddenly smirked as he looked at Seb and Tom. "Whatever. I'm outta here. Oh, and Seb? Just wait 'til the parents hear about this. What do you think I should tell them? I mean, why *is* Tom here?"

Josh pushed passed Tom and walked out the front door, not bothering to close it. Tom watched as he climbed into his car and drove away, but not before he gave a sarcastic smile and wave at them.

Tom turned to Seb, but didn't know what to say. What would Josh say to his parents? How would that affect them? Seb walked into the lounge and picked up his phone, dialling a number.

"Hi, Mum. I need you to listen to me for a minute. I'm with Tom, you know Josh's old friend. Remember I told you I'd seen him recently. Well, Josh has just been here, and it turns out he was the baby's father and not Tom. No, just listen. Tom's moving in with me."

Tom watched stunned as Seb told his mum.

"No, Mum, I'm not doing it to upset you... No, Mum. He's moving in with me...I don't see how that affects you or Dad...Look, I can tell you're upset...alright, I'll give you time to get used to it." Seb suddenly stared at his phone before turning to Tom. "Well, that went well. She hung up on me."

"You didn't have to tell them. You don't know that Josh will say anything."

Seb looked at him with a look that clearly spoke that he thought Tom was being naive. "You know fine well Josh will say something. I bet he's going straight round there now. He's always been like this, always had to be better than me. I don't understand the reason for his jealousy. I've never been treated any better than him. He was always the one that Mum and Dad did everything for, and I had no problem with that. He's my little brother."

"Not so little anymore."

"No, I guess not. I just don't remember him being like this."

"You weren't around much, remember? You were at Uni? He could be a right bastard at times, but he was fun, ya know. He was a good mate to me, well, until the end, but he did have that ego." Tom chuckled as he remembered the good times they'd had together. "He was always up for a laugh. Don't get me wrong, we did shit we shouldn't have, but we were young and daft and thought we could get away with anything. But he did have this darkness to him."

"I should have seen something. You're only five years younger than me, so you were what? Thirteen or fourteen when I went to Uni?"

"Yeah. Five years makes a lot of difference. He used to say how proud your parents were of you goin' to Uni." Tom sighed. "I don't know what more we can do about this, do you?"

"Doesn't matter now, does it? My parents know you're moving in. Let them think what they want."

Tom watched as Seb sat and stared at his hands, his face showing no expression. Tom walked into the kitchen and filled the kettle before turning it on. Grabbing some cups, he put the teabags in and waited for the kettle to boil. Tom stood watching it, unsure as to what to say to Seb to make the situation better. Not only had Josh found out, but Seb had been forced to tell his parents about him. Well, not the exact nature of their relationship, but that he was around. He wasn't sure how Seb would feel about all of this now. Once the reality had sunk in, he wouldn't be surprised if Seb asked him not to move in with him.

When he heard the kettle boil, he filled the cups with water then went to the fridge to get the milk. Once the tea was made, he walked into the lounge and handed one to Seb, then sat down next to him on the sofa.

"I don't have to move in. You could phone your parents and tell them you've changed your mind. I don't want you to fall out with them over this."

"Is that what you want?" Seb turned and looked at him, and Tom could see that Seb had been hurt by what he'd said.

"No, not really. I just feel so bad for what's happening now. If you hadn't seen me that night, none of this would be happening."

He watched as Seb looked away. Was Seb thinking the same thing?

"I searched for you, remember? I've done that a number of times now." Seb stood and paced in front of Tom. "Do I wish I could be with you and my parents be okay with it? Course I do, but I don't think that's how it's going to be, well, not at first. Give them time and I know they'll change their minds eventually. If they don't, well, it's their loss. I can't hide who I am from them forever. I've had boyfriends and not been able to tell them or bring them home." Seb walked over to the window and stared out. "I always knew one day that it could be a possibility that the person I'd want to settle down with would be male so I've known that this would happen. They have to decide if they can accept me for who I am or not. I'm not doing anything wrong here. I haven't committed a crime. I just happen to love someone who's male. They can deal with it or not. I guess you could say I made peace with that a long time ago. Sure, I thought about it more so recently when I found you again and yeah, I did think hard before asking you but this is my life, and you only have one chance to live it."

"You love me?" Tom asked him. It had only been a few weeks since they had met up again, and even though he knew he had strong feelings for Seb, he didn't know that Seb felt that way for him.

"I think I've loved you for a long time now. That was part of why I looked for you that first time and why I couldn't stay away now. I don't expect you to say it back, Tom. I just wanted you to know that that's how I feel. Now, I know we agreed we would get your things, but after Josh's little visit, I fancy a drink. Do you mind waiting 'til tomorrow?"

"No, and I think I need one as well."

"Come on then, I'll see what I've got in, and we can have a drink while I cook."

Tom held his hand over his heart and looked at Seb with at him. "What? You don't want me to cook?"

Seb smiled, walking over to where Tom sat. He leaned over Tom and bent down to kiss him. "I do want to eat at some time tonight. Something edible with no risk of food poisoning."

Tom laughed against his mouth as he reached up to kiss him back. "Well, I guess I'll have time to learn now, won't I?"

They walked into the kitchen, and Seb opened the freezer and took out a couple of pizza boxes, holding them up for Tom to see. Tom nodded as he grabbed a couple of beers from the fridge, popping them open.

"Right, says fifteen to twenty minutes. So, what should we do to pass the time?"

Seeing the look on Seb's face, Tom chuckled. "Got some ideas?"

Leaning against the counter, Seb reached for him, pulling him close. Tom settled in between Seb's legs, kissing him as he wrapped his arms around Seb's waist. They stayed like that, not rushing anything, and Tom enjoyed it. Having never really kissed anyone, he loved spending time doing it with Seb and it helped that Seb knew how to kiss.

The timer went off, and Seb checked the food and Tom got the plates out. They sliced the pizza, grabbed some more beers and went into the lounge to eat. After finishing, Tom cleared up, and as he walked back into the lounge, heard the phone go. He watched as Seb reached over to answer it, hoping it wasn't Josh or his parents.

"Hello. Oh, hi Mum--"

Tom figured hoping wasn't good enough. He sat down as he listened to Seb talk.

"Well, if you want to believe Josh...He was only here for five minutes!...What?...Yeah right, Josh who has never done a thing wrong...You know what, fine...Look, I love you both, but it's my choice. Deal with it."

Tom watched as Seb slammed the phone down and dropped his head in his hands as he growled. He didn't know what to say to make the situation any better so decided to stay silent.

Seb turned and looked at him before he spoke, and Tom could hear how upset he was. "They told me never to come back. They don't want anything to do with a faggot loving bastard. Nice, right?"

"I'm so sorry, Seb. I don't have to--"

"No, I've told you, you're staying." Seb interrupted him. "I've made my choice. This is my life, and I want you in it. If that means going through this shit, then that's what I'll do, but I'm not losing you again." Seb paused as he looked at Tom. "You do want to be here? No bullshit."

Tom swallowed before he nodded his head. "Yeah, I do."

Seb nodded as he looked away and stared out the window. Tom

watched him, again struggling to find something to say, the right words to make Seb feel a little better. But, what was there to say? Seb's parents had decided to disown him because of Tom, and he knew how that felt. It hurt like hell. It felt like a crushing weight on your chest and you couldn't breathe properly. He moved closer to Seb and leaned against him, letting him know he was there. Seb smiled at him before he reached around and hugged him tight to his side.

"This isn't your fault, Tom. Don't ever think it is. I made this decision. I could have lied and kept us a secret, but neither of us would have been happy. This is the way it has to be for now."

Tom stood and reached down, grabbing Seb's hand and pulling him up. "Come on, let's go to bed. We can clean up tomorrow. It feels like this day has lasted forever."

Tom pulled Seb behind him as he walked upstairs. Once he walked into their room, he quickly stripped down to his boxers and then helped Seb do the same. They took turns using the bathroom then crawled under the covers. Tom lay on his side as he felt Seb spoon him. Considering everything that had happened that day, it didn't take long for him to fall asleep.

Chapter Eighteen

Seb woke, blinking to clear the sleep from his eyes. He could feel Tom curled up next to him, and twisting his head to the side, confirmed Tom was still asleep. Seb looked up at the ceiling and sighed remembering the events of yesterday.

Josh had gone back to their parents and had told them everything he'd seen and added a bit more just for the fun of it, insinuating that he'd interrupted them having sex. Now they knew that Tom was moving in. Seb would have liked to have some time alone with Tom before he had to tell his parents, but Josh wouldn't let an opportunity like that pass him by. Maybe Tom was right. Maybe he had missed the change in Josh, but when he looked at him, he still saw his kid brother, the boy he needed to look out for and protect. But somewhere along the way, the boy had started to grow into a man, and that man didn't seem like the type of person Seb would want to know.

Seb couldn't think of anything he'd done to cause Josh to act the way he did towards him. He'd always been there for him when he could. Yes, that hadn't been as often as it was after he went to Uni, but he'd tried. Listening to Tom describe Josh made him realise that he didn't know his brother at all.

His parents wanted nothing to do with him now. The things they had screamed at him about his relationship with Tom were things he would never tell Tom. He didn't need to hear their hatred. He'd come a long way since Seb had seen him on that street, and Seb didn't want all that hard work to have been for nothing.

Yes, they had a bump in the road when Adam had been found dead, but overall, Tom was better. He wanted Tom to have the best life possible, even though he knew it would take him a long time to get over the past four years. He wanted to show him all the good things in life. Go away on holidays together, be there to celebrate birthdays and Christmases, all the important events. Tom deserved that.

Seb looked at the clock and saw that it was almost eight. If he didn't get up, he'd be late for work, and this was the last week before Christmas. All his cases needed to be up to date in case any new information came to light. He slipped from the bed as quietly as he could and walked to the bathroom to get ready.

When he walked back into the bedroom, he found Tom awake looking at him.

"Morning," Tom mumbled. "Guess you're getting ready for work."

Seb nodded as he pulled a suit out from the wardrobe. "Yeah. I can drop you off on my way in if you want. We can meet up for lunch too."

He watched as Tom pulled the covers back and stood before stretching. Seb stopped getting dressed so that he could stare at him. Tom still needed to put some weight on, but he wasn't quite as thin as he'd been when they'd first met.

Tom smirked at him as he caught him staring, then walked over and kissed him on the cheek. He watched him as he walked into the bathroom. The back was just as good as the front.

Staring at his erection, Seb sighed. Shame to waste it, but they didn't have the time. He finished dressing and went downstairs to get breakfast started, glancing at the clock as he did. Shit, he was going to be late if he didn't get moving.

As Seb made coffee, he heard Tom come down the stairs and walk into the kitchen. "Breakfast?"

Tom nodded and grabbed some toast off the plate. "Still alright to drop me off?"

"Yeah, if we hurry. I kind of overslept."

"Oh, in that case, I can walk."

"No, I can drop you off, but I'm pushing it. Get that coffee down you and we can finish the toast in the car."

"Okay."

They drank their coffee, Seb burning his throat in the process, then grabbed their toast and coats and headed out. Seb locked the door behind them as Tom got in the car. He backed off the drive and then drove in the direction of Tom's.

"Here, you'll need these for later," Seb explained as he handed some keys over to him. "Also take this for the taxi when you bring your things back."

"You don't have to give me money," Tom grumbled.

"I know, but we're living together now and until you decide what you're going to do, I'm going to help you out." Seb held a hand up when Tom attempted to interrupt him. "Don't think I'm trying to say that you can't support yourself, because I'm not and I'm not trying to demean you in any way. Just let me help right now until you know what it is you want to do. Please."

"Sorry. I guess I'm still a little touchy about it. Thanks."

Seb turned into the street where the house was that Tom had been squatting in and pulled over, shutting the engine off. He turned to him and asked, "You ready?"

Tom looked at the abandoned house, the house he had called home, before looking back at Seb and nodding. "Yeah. I'm ready. I'll see you later." Seb leaned over and kissed Tom before he got out of the car and walked round the back.

Starting the engine, Seb glanced over his shoulder before pulling away from the pavement. He checked the clock and swore when he realised that he was going to be late and hoped that Geoff wouldn't be too pissed at him. He could explain what was going on, Geoff knew enough of the details, and he could work the time back later.

By the time he walked into the office, he was only ten minutes late, but the first person he ran into was his boss. Geoff looked at him before speaking. "When you have a minute, my office please."

Seb watched Geoff walk back to his office before he rushed over to his work area and quickly took his coat off and put his case on the floor. Running a hand through his hair, he walked over to Geoff's office, noticing his secretary wasn't there.

Knocking on the door, he walked in, and seeing Geoff was on the phone, stood waiting. Geoff looked up and pointed to the chair in front of his desk. Seb sat down and waited, feeling like a naughty schoolboy in front of the headmaster, waiting for his punishment. He hated feeling that way; he was a grown man, for fuck's sake. All he had to do was explain what had happened, and it would be fine. He moved his hand from his mouth when he realised he was chewing his thumbnail and wiped the palms of his now sweaty hands against his pants.

He watched as Geoff wrapped up the call and placed the phone back down. Geoff looked at him for a minute before speaking. "How's you weekend been? Good?"

"Er, alright for the most part. Why?"

"I had a call yesterday. From your parents. Want to tell me why they would be phoning me about their adult son?"

Seb's jaw dropped as he stared at Geoff. His parents had phoned his boss? At his home? What the fuck! He shook his head in utter disbelief at what he was hearing. They'd gone too far by phoning Geoff.

"It doesn't matter, Seb, and you don't have to explain anything to me. I heard it all. So this Tom is moving in with you, and your parents aren't happy about it. You are of age, right?" Geoff smirked at him, but Seb failed to see how any of this was remotely amusing. It was mortifying!

"I am so, so sorry they phoned you. I can't believe they did that!" Seb groaned as he dropped his head in his hands.

"Don't worry about it. We talked about all of this, so I'm aware of the situation. Your parents aren't exactly welcoming Tom with open arms, are they. From what I could gather, they believe he's making you gay. I wasn't too happy with that, so I politely asked them not to include me in your personal life and hung up. I won't have anyone's sexuality discussed like that around me. What you do in your private life is up to you, well, unless it's illegal. Then I will fire you," Geoff advised as he smiled at him.

"I can't understand why they would call you unless they thought you'd fire me or something." Seb stared at Geoff, horrified. "They asked you to speak to me about it, didn't they? Get me to change my mind or I'd lose my job."

"It doesn't matter what they said. Your job is safe here. You're a damn good worker, and I'm not going to fire you for helping a friend out, regardless of the nature of your relationship. Now let's get down to

Take a Chance

business. I need you to get on the Walters case and provide me with an outline by lunch. Alright?" Geoff pointed to a file on his desk.

"Sure, okay," Seb answered, blinking rapidly at the sudden change in subject matter. "I'll get right on it."

Geoff nodded as he looked down at a report on his desk. "Can you close the door on your way out, please?"

Seb picked up the file and walked out, closing the door behind him. He walked over to his desk and sat heavily, exhaling hard as he stared out the window. He shook his head as he thought about the reasons why his parents had phoned. It was disgusting to think his parents would pull a stunt like that. They could have gotten him fired. Was that what they wanted? Just because Tom was moving in with him. It was his life, his home and his choice, and he was choosing Tom.

For the next couple of hours, Seb struggled to read the information presented to him regarding the case. He found he had to reread paragraphs repeatedly as he wasn't taking in any of the details he had read. He sighed as he threw the paperwork on the desk and looked at the time. Shit! He only had an hour to get the initial outline ready, and at the rate he was going, he would probably need a week!

Somehow he managed to get the work completed, and as he was on his way to hand it over to Geoff, he heard his name shouted from the reception area. Walking over he was surprised to see Tom and Geoff stood there.

"What's wrong?"

Tom walked over to him, and Seb could see the fear and worry etched on his face, his skin pale, and Tom was wringing his hands. "Ben's missing. I've looked everywhere for him, but I can't find him. This isn't like him. He's very careful." Tom stressed the word as he spoke.

"Have you been to the police?" Seb asked.

Tom snorted as he looked away. "What do you think?"

"I'm on lunch soon. I'll get my car, and we can look for him, okay?" Seb turned to Geoff. "I have to help."

Geoff nodded his agreement. "Do you know where he might have gone?" he asked Tom.

Tom frowned at Geoff before he answered him. "I've searched everywhere I could think of."

Seb suddenly thought of a place Tom might not have gone. "What about where we found Adam?"

Tom looked confused at the question. "Why would he go there? There's nothing there for him to see."

"But it's where Adam died, and you told me he'd been feeling guilty about it even though it wasn't his fault. You stated they'd always worked together."

Tom glanced at Geoff before looking at Seb. "We can talk about that outside."

"I know," Geoff murmured to Tom.

Tom look startled, eyes widening, lips parting slightly. He turned and looked back at Seb. "You told him? About me? About what I do?"

Before waiting for Seb to answer, Tom stormed out of the reception area and walked to the lift. Seb followed him and grabbed his arm, pulling him around to face him.

"I understand you're angry at me, but let me help you. We can talk about this after we've found him."

Tom pulled his arm away angrily, "Fuck off. I trusted you. I don't need your help. Forget I came."

"I made him tell me," Geoff informed from behind them. "He didn't want to say anything, but I could see something was wrong, and it was affecting his work. I'm the one you need to blame, not Seb."

"Really? What did you do? Threaten to fire him? You're the boss, right?"

"Yes, I am the boss, and no, I didn't threaten to fire him. But he is an employee, and I don't like to see my employees the way he was. He needed someone to talk to, and he couldn't find you."

Tom looked away before muttering, "I needed to sort things out."

"No, you needed to get drunk." Seb sighed as he rubbed the back of his neck. "Look, let's find Ben and you can shout at me later."

"Go. Don't come back until you've found him. Call me." Geoff turned and walked back into the reception, leaving Tom and Seb standing there, staring at each other. The stare was broken when the elevator pinged, announcing it had arrived on their floor. They both got in, and Seb pressed for the ground floor.

"We'll get my car and go to where we found Adam."

Tom had his arms crossed over his chest, refusing to look at Seb. "Yeah, you might be right," he admitted. "I hate thinking he might have gone there though."

"You've checked all the usual places he worked, right? So, that just leaves the ones you wouldn't consider. He's probably there and more than likely drunk or sleeping it off."

"I hope you're right, I really do," Tom muttered as he chewed worryingly on his bottom lip.

They exited the lift, and Seb walked over to where he'd parked his car. They both got in, and Seb drove to the warehouse where they had found Adam's body. With the weather and traffic, it took almost an hour to get there.

Seb pulled up outside and looked at the building. He could still see remnants of the police tape on the door, but the rest looked like it had been pulled off. It also looked like they had boarded the place off, but Seb could see where the boarding was removed.

Getting out of the car, they walked over to the door and Seb pulled the board back while Tom ducked and went in. Seb followed and stood just inside. It was virtually pitch black inside, the only light coming from the roof, and as it was so dark and dreary outside, that wasn't much. He could see shapes and hear people whispering around them. He could feel eyes on him and shivered uncontrollably.

"Let's go," Seb told him.

Seb led the way to the back of the building with Tom following. He didn't want to stay in this place a minute longer than necessary. Seb was walking straight to the room they'd found Adam's body when he heard Tom gasp behind him.

Turning back towards Tom, Seb walked into another room, smaller than the one Adam had been found in. At first, he couldn't see what he was looking at, but as his eyes focused, he could make out someone lying on the floor. For a second, he thought it was another dead body, and he could feel the churning in his stomach, but then he heard a small groan.

"It's Ben," Tom whispered as he walked further into the room and knelt beside him.

Seb sagged against the wall in relief, realising Ben was still alive and more than likely sleeping off the alcohol. But that changed when he heard Tom swear.

"What? What is it?" Seb asked, pushing of the wall and taking a couple of steps towards Tom.

Tom picked up some empty packets and showed Seb. Paracetamol.

"Fuck! I'll call an ambulance. How many packets are there? Is there any booze?"

Tom nodded to both questions. "Looks like two packets and a bottle of whisky."

Seb dialled emergency services and quickly explained the situation and their location. Once he got off the phone, he called Geoff.

"Hello, Geoff Foster."

"It's me, Seb. We've found him, but it isn't good. It looks like he's tried to kill himself."

"Where are you and have you phoned for an ambulance?"

"Yeah, an ambulance is on its way now. We're at the place we found Adam's body."

"You were right then. Is he conscious?" Geoff asked him.

"Tom's trying to get him to wake up now. Shit, he doesn't need this on top of everything else."

"I know. Look, call me when you know where you're going, and I'll come over."

"Thanks, Geoff, but you don't need to do that. You've done enough already."

"No, you two have been through hell already, and with the situation with your parents, you need all the support you can get, Seb. Call me and tell me where you'll be going."

Seb stared at the phone as Geoff hung up. He cocked his head slightly as he heard a siren in the distance. He listened for a minute, realising it was getting closer.

"Tom, the ambulance is coming. I'll go outside and meet them, okay?"

Tom nodded but continued to try and get Ben to wake up by shaking him and saying his name. Seb walked out to the building as quickly as he could. Shit, Tom didn't need this. Not with Adam's murder. Fuck, Ben needed to live. Seb rubbed his hands over his face as he waited outside. Within minutes he saw the flashing lights and waved his arms to get the driver's attention.

He explained the situation as he led the paramedics into the room where Ben lay. Tom stood and walked over to Seb, grabbing his hand as they watched the paramedics go to work. They answered the questions as best they could when asked, but it still seemed to take forever before they were putting him on a stretcher and were trying to get him out of the building. It wasn't an easy job with the debris scattered around, but as they neared the door, both Seb and Tom pulled the boarding away to allow them to exit.

"Do you want to go in the ambulance with him?" Seb asked Tom as they loaded Ben onto the ambulance.

"Yeah," Tom answered as he watched Ben from outside.

Seb nodded. He knew Tom would go with Ben. "Alright, I'll follow behind and meet you there."

"Shit. Matt and Luke don't know. I left them at the house."

"I'll get them and bring them with me, alright? Now go, they're not going to wait for you."

Seb got into his car and watched the ambulance move off before he phoned Geoff.

"Hi, it's Seb. We're heading to Manchester Royal. Should be there in ten minutes or so."

"Okay, I'll meet there."

Seb threw the phone on the passenger seat as he started his car and drove to the house. God, he hoped Ben was OK. Tom didn't need another one of his friends to die. He'd had enough to deal with. He pulled up outside and ran around the back. As he entered, he shouted out, "Matt, Luke. It's Seb, Tom's friend. We've found Ben."

Take a Chance

"Where is he?" the blond one asked him as he walked out from the living room.

"On his way to the hospital. It looks like he tried to kill himself. Come on, I'll take you now."

They both followed him out, and before long, Seb was driving to the hospital. He answered their questions, explaining that he didn't know a lot other than what they'd found at the warehouse. They all eventually sat in silence as Seb drove through the streets, the air thick as tension built in the car. When he got to the hospital, he parked as close as he could, paid for the parking and then ran to catch up to the other two. They walked into to A and E, and Seb was surprised to see Geoff already there, sitting next to Tom.

"Well, what now?" Seb asked as he approached them.

"Now we wait," Geoff answered.

Chapter Nineteen

Tom sat watching the people come and go. God, it was a depressing place. Busy, but so quiet. Even at this time of the day the staff were dealing with drunks, people who didn't appear to want any help but wouldn't leave either. Suddenly, Tom heard screaming and security came running in to assist with one man who was trying to attack a nurse. Tom shook his head. It must be difficult to work here at times, and he admired the staff that did.

Thinking of Ben, Tom dropped his head in his hands. He didn't even know his surname, none of them did, but it was something he was going to change. They couldn't be in this situation again. Tom stood and paced the reception area. He couldn't sit still. He had to be doing something even if it was walking around aimlessly. He'd answered the paramedic's questions in the ambulance and then Matt and Luke's. All he'd been able to tell them was pretty much the same thing that Seb had told the paramedics when they had been called out.

Take a Chance

After pacing for a few minutes, Tom slumped back in his chair. He turned and looked at Seb when he felt his hand rub his back. He wasn't sure why Seb's boss had stayed. He didn't know Ben, but he had to admit it was a relief, and he didn't feel so alone. He wasn't sure how long he could hold it together for, especially with Matt and Luke being there too. They both looked devastated at what had happened. So much had changed in such a short period of time, and now he didn't know what to do. Should he stay with them or move in with Seb as he'd planned? That would mean leaving them on their own because he didn't know what was going to happen to Ben after this. He didn't even know if he would survive.

When Tom heard the double doors that led to the triage area, Tom glanced over.

"Geoff Foster," a male nurse spoke.

"That's me," Geoff replied as he stood.

"Can you come with me, please?"

Geoff looked at the others sat there. "Can they all come?"

"Sorry, only two people at a time."

"Come on, Tom. You mind waiting here, Seb?"

"No, I'll keep these guys company," Seb answered.

"Just come out and tell us how he is," Matt shouted at them as they walked away.

Tom followed Geoff and the nurse through the doors and down a corridor. People hurried past them, nurses and other visitors, as they walked into a large room that had several curtained off areas. The nurse stopped at one of these areas and pulled the curtain back, revealing Ben lying on his side in bed. He had wires attached to him everywhere, and Tom took a second to pause and just stare at him, gasping at the condition he was in.

"We were lucky. It doesn't look like he'd taken a lot of drugs before you found him, but we will continue to monitor him for the next twenty-four hours. Do you know where he'll be staying when he leaves? We have him listed as no fixed abode."

"He'll stay with me," Geoff answered.

Tom looked at him, mouth dropping open. He didn't know Ben, so why would he help him?

"Alright, if you can come over with me, I'll take some details. We can discuss everything there."

Tom watched as Geoff followed the nurse out of the cubicle. He walked over and pulled the curtain closed, sealing him in with Ben. He looked down at him as the lay on the bed, noticing how small he seemed. He didn't look good at all. His eyes appeared sunken, and his skin had no colour to it.

Tom pulled a chair over and sat next to Ben, watching him breathe. He looked up at the monitors, understanding some of the information displayed but not all. He felt drained as he sat there, thinking about how lucky they'd been to find him in time. Ben must have sat there for a long time, thinking about ending his life. From what the nurse had explained, he hadn't taken a lot so maybe this was a cry for help. What the fuck did he know? He wasn't a shrink and Ben hadn't talked about how he was feeling. Yeah, he knew that Ben felt guilty about Adam, they all did, but he never knew it went this deep and he would try to end his life.

He turned when he heard the curtain being pulled back to find Matt standing there.

"Geoff came out and told us what the nurse said." He walked over to where there was another chair and sat down on the opposite side of the bed to Tom. "Do you think he'll stay with this Geoff? I'm not sure if that's a good thing or not. We don't know him, do we?"

Take a Chance

"Seb does. Geoff's his boss, so they must know each other well. Why else would he have come here?" Tom sighed. "I'm not sure either, but he needs to be off the streets. He needs to have someone watching him."

Matt reached over and held Ben's hand as he looked at him. "Seb asked Luke and me to move in. Did you speak to him?"

Tom quickly glanced up. It wasn't something he thought Seb would do. Seb knew how he felt about leaving them, and Tom understood the cost to Seb, so he never thought he would offer them a place to stay. Then again, he never thought Ben would try to commit suicide.

"Are you gonna move in?" he asked Matt.

"I'm not sure. We would be stupid not to, right? Off the streets, not having to do what we do. But we have no money, so how would we pay? Rent, bills, food." Matt shook his head. "I want to accept, if not for me then definitely for Luke, but I don't have anything to give him. Will he let us stay and not pay?" Matt bit his lip, glancing over at Tom before looking back at Ben.

"He knows the situation, so I don't think he would have offered if he expected you to pay. And I'm certain Geoff would help. He's going to take care of Ben, isn't he? Stay, take the time to figure shit out." Tom stood up and stretched. "I'll go and let Luke come in. When he's moved to the wards, I don't know if we will be able to stay with him."

Tom left the cubicle and walked to the waiting area, sighing as he rubbed the back of his neck. The muscles ached. As soon as Luke saw him, he was out of the chair and walking through the doors. Tom sat next to Seb and leaned his head on his shoulder. It was only then he realised that Geoff wasn't there.

"Hey, where's your boss?"

"He's left to get things ready for when Ben's released. What do you think he'll do? Do you think Ben will stay with Geoff?"

Tom shrugged. "I hope so. He needs to be off the streets. He's obviously in a dark place right now, isn't he? He wouldn't have tried to kill himself otherwise." Tom paused then added, "Thanks for asking Luke and Matt to stay. You didn't have to."

"Course I did. I couldn't leave them to fend for themselves. Luke seems so young. Far too young to be out on the streets."

"Matt's worried about money."

"Yeah, I told him not to be, but I guess you've all depended for so long on each other that it must be hard to let someone in and help. I know Geoff is willing to help too." Seb sighed. "Hard to trust."

"Yeah, it's hard to trust, but you knew that with me. I've not been easy."

"Still not." Seb smiled at him. "You're worth it though. I know things won't be easy, but I'm here."

Tom didn't say anything as he sat watching people in the waiting area. Sometime later, Matt and Luke came out and told them Ben was being moved to another ward for further monitoring and that they could come back tomorrow during visiting hours.

"Let's go get all your things. Have you got much?" Seb asked as they left the hospital and walked to his car.

Both Matt and Luke said no as they got into Seb's car. He drove straight to the house they'd been living in, and it didn't take long for them to pack everything up and, after one final check, leave.

Tom watched the streets go by as they sat in the car. No one was speaking, but he wasn't surprised. It had been an emotional day for all of them. For Tom, it felt like the last few weeks had been an emotional roller coaster ride, one he was happy to get off. He was pulled from his thoughts when Seb turned onto his driveway and switched the engine off.

"Come on, let's get everything in and I'll order some takeout. Don't feel like cooking tonight."

Tom carried his bag in, which contained everything he owned, and took it to his bedroom. It seemed strange standing there knowing this was his and Seb's room now. He opened the bag and looked at what little belongings he had. He rummaged through his bag and considered throwing most of it away. He didn't have many clothes, and the ones he had brought back with him were one good wash away from falling apart. Thank fuck Seb had bought him some new ones because he didn't think these would have lasted much longer.

"You can wash them if you want," he heard Seb say behind him.

"I'm thinking of just throwing them out. A good wash would kill them off."

Seb chuckled as he walked over to him and hugged him from behind. "How're you feeling?"

"Really?" Tom felt Seb nod before he continued. "Strange. Tired. Numb, I think." Tom shrugged. "Everything's changing, and I'm just trying to keep up."

"Yeah, I can understand that. I'll leave you with this and go and order. The guys want pizza. Okay with you?"

"Yeah, that's great, thanks."

Tom watched Seb walk out of the bedroom and sat heavily on the bed. Hearing the shower start, Tom realised both Matt and Luke would be taking the opportunity to get clean. He understood that feeling.

Tom sighed. Yeah, lots had changed. He still felt guilty as hell with the mess Seb had to face with his parents, but he wanted to be here with him. He loved him. When it had happened, he didn't know, but he had fallen for him. Maybe it had started when he was younger with that silly crush he'd had, and now it had grown. He had wanted to say something to Seb when he had told him, but for some reason, he'd kept it back. Not because Seb said he didn't have to say it, but maybe because he was still expecting to wake up and find that this had all been a dream. He never once thought that he would find a way out of the life he'd been living. He'd wanted to, but he never could see a way, and now Seb was here and had pulled him free. Not just him though; Matt and Luke had a chance too now.

He stood and picked his bag up, quickly searched through it for a couple of items he wanted to keep, and then took the bag and walked downstairs with it. Seb watched him as he went outside and threw it in the bin. He closed the lid and stood staring at it before inhaling deeply and turning away. That part of his life was finally over.

Walking back in, he found everyone in the living room watching TV. He sat down next to Seb on the sofa, leaning into him. "I've just spoken to Geoff. It looks like they might be keeping Ben in longer than we thought. Something to do with his blood work. I've got the next couple of days off to get everything sorted out here," Seb told him.

"Oh, okay," Tom muttered as he suddenly yawned.

"So I thought we'd go shopping tomorrow. I'm pretty sure you all need things, right?"

Tom, as well as Matt and Luke, voiced their denials, but Seb just smiled at them.

"I know Tom doesn't need much, but I also know you two could use some new clothes and other things, so we'll do it tomorrow. If it's a question of money, don't worry about it. I'm not loaded, but I'm not skint either and Geoff explained he wanted to help too. So just accept it as a gift for now."

"I don't think I can. You're already letting us stay here for free. I just don't feel comfortable with it," Matt argued.

"Alright, so how about when you're on your feet and you know what you're doing, we can look at you paying me back then or even pay it forward. If someone else is in need, you can help them."

"Matt, just accept it. I know how hard it is to accept that someone is doing something for you and not wanting anything in return. Seb isn't like that," Tom explained to him.

Matt turned and looked at Luke, who smiled back at him and gave a slight nod. "Okay, thanks."

Tom sat listening to the others ask Seb questions about his job and his plans for the house. They only stopped when the food arrived. They ate quickly, and it wasn't long before they all went upstairs for the night.

Tom crawled into bed, suddenly feeling the day catch up with him. He felt exhausted. He lay there while he waited for Seb and turned to face him when he walked in.

"Thank you for today," he murmured as he watched Seb undress.

"Nothing to thank me for, Tom. Anyone would have helped."

Tom snorted. "No. Not just anyone would have helped. I guess it's just who you are. You like to help people, even when they don't seem to want it."

Tom turned on his side as Seb got into bed and then cuddled into him. He sighed as he kissed Seb's neck. Tom felt Seb move over him, and he rolled onto his back, opening his legs so Seb could settle in between them. Seb leaned down to kiss Tom gently, a series of soft touches to his lips before he sucked his bottom lip. Tom opened his mouth, and they kissed slowly, languidly. Tom felt Seb's erection as their cocks touched, moaning at the contact.

They continued to kiss, hands gently touching each other's bodies. Seb rubbed their cocks together and it wasn't long until Tom wanted more.

"Take them off," he muttered between kisses.

"Are you sure?" Seb asked, licking across Tom's lips.

"Yeah, I am."

Seb sat up and pulled his boxer briefs down and off. He then did the same to Tom's, watching as Tom's dick bounced back, hitting his abdomen. He lay back over Tom and kissed him again. Tom heard the click of a bottle opening and then felt Seb fingers rim his hole before one slowly pushed in. Tom moaned as Seb pushed his finger in and out before adding a second one and twisting them until he hit his prostate. Tom gasped and moaned louder. Every time Seb pushed his fingers and rubbed that spot, Tom hitched his hips. He couldn't stop moving and moaning. When Seb added a third, Tom thought he was about to explode.

"God, Seb, fuck me now!" he begged.

Tom watched as Seb opened the condom wrapper and rolled it on, then coated it in lube. Tom spread his legs and felt Seb rub the head of his cock around his hole before slowly pushing in, breaking past the ring of muscle. Seb didn't stop until he was fully in, and his balls nestled against Tom's arse.

Seb lowered himself onto Tom and slowly kissed him as he began to move in and out of Tom's body. Tom bent his knees and wrapped his legs around Seb's waist as he lifted his hips to meet Seb's thrusts. Seb's hands never stopped moving over Tom's body, touching everywhere he could reach. Tom had never felt like this before; this wasn't just sex between them now. Tom could feel the emotions rushing through him as Seb continued to move.

Tom looked up into Seb's hazel eyes. "I love you," he whispered before pulling Seb's head down to kiss him again. Tom knew Seb had heard him as he started to move faster and harder in him.

"I love you too," Seb groaned. Seb pushed a hand in between their bodies and grabbed Tom's cock, stroking it as he increased the speed of his thrusts.

Gasping, Tom's legs jerked, his balls pulling up tight to his body. Tingling radiated from his balls, along his dick and channel. Pressure built until Tom couldn't hold back anymore. He arched his back as he started to shoot over his stomach and chest. Electricity raced through his body as it jerked uncontrollably.

Seb stiffened above him before he cried out as he came.

Tom shivered as his body calmed, loosening his grip on Seb. Seb nestled his face in Tom's neck and kissed him, rubbing his hands up and down Tom's arms.

"Are you alright?" Seb asked eventually when they were both breathing better.

"Yeah." Tom swallowed, turning his face towards Seb and kissing his cheek.

Seb raised up onto his forearms, smiled then kissed Tom before slowly pulling out and removing the condom, throwing it into the bin next to the bed. He grabbed some wet wipes from the drawer and cleaned Tom up. Tom moved over slightly as Seb lay back down next to him and rested his head next to Tom's on the pillows.

Tom suddenly yawned and then smiled sheepishly. "Sorry. I'm really tired."

"It's okay. It's been a long, difficult day, hasn't it?"

"It has."

"Come on, let's get some sleep and see how everything is in the morning."

Tom rolled over and felt Seb do the same, spooning him from behind. It wasn't long before he was asleep.

The next few days passed by in a blur. They all went into the city, and Seb bought Matt and Luke what they needed. They argued over the purchases, but Seb got his way eventually. They ate out for lunch and by mid-afternoon, Seb got a call from Geoff telling them he would be picking Ben up that night. Apparently, Ben hadn't said anything about staying with Geoff, but Tom was waiting for Ben to say something. It wasn't like Ben not to say what he wanted. Geoff had asked that they give Ben a couple of days to settle in before going over to see him, and even though Tom wasn't impressed by that, he understood the reasons behind the request.

Seb went back to work, and the three of them started to adjust to the changes in their lives. They visited Ben, but he didn't seem interested in talking. It was almost like he had fallen into a depression. He seemed like a vacant shell. Tom tried to look on the bright side. At least Ben wasn't on the streets anymore. None of them were. Ben was in a much better place now and hopefully he'd be able to get over what had happened.

There was some talk of Ben seeing a counsellor, but it was too soon to know if he would do that or not. As Tom got to know Geoff, he found he liked him and that he was as Seb had told him, a good guy. He came from a loving family that had no issues with his sexuality and Tom learned that Geoff was taking over the solicitors now that his father was reducing his hours.

Geoff was attracted to Ben, and it was obvious to Tom; the looks he gave him and the occasional touches, but Ben seemed oblivious to it. Geoff had a hard road ahead of him if he wanted any form of relationship with Ben.

Christmas came around, and Tom couldn't help but get excited

Take a Chance

about opening the presents under the tree. He hadn't been able to get Seb much, but Seb had commented that he had what he wanted with Tom. Seb seemed a little down throughout the day, and Tom had done his best to try and keep him happy. Seb's family still hadn't come around to the fact that Tom was there and hadn't responded to any of Seb's calls.

Seb had gone round to see them and try to sort things out, but when he'd returned, Tom knew he hadn't gotten anywhere. Seb had given him a grim smile when he'd come back and shook his head, indicating that his parents hadn't been accepting of his relationship with Tom.

Tom had begun to think about what he was going to do with his life now that it wasn't a constant struggle to survive. Seb was supportive of him, well, all three of them, and Tom wanted to be able to do something positive now. He looked into finishing his education. If he wanted a decent job, he needed to have a good education, but he wasn't sure what in. He hadn't thought about it for so long now that when he knew he could do something, he felt overwhelmed. He'd heard Matt and Luke discussing college and he knew that was something he wanted to do.

As he sat there one night watching Seb make dinner for them, laughing and joking with Matt and Luke, he finally felt like he had found home. The journey had been a difficult one, and he knew there would be ups and downs in the future, but he finally felt happy.

He stood up and walked up to Seb, kissing him softly. "I love you."

"I love you too."

The End

Megs Pritchard

Sneak peek at New Beginnings
Book Two in the Second Chances Series

Geoff Foster sat in his study, finishing the summary of an ongoing case. It still needed some more touches, but he was finally close to finishing the first draft of his closing argument and, as lead solicitor, it needed to be strong.

When Geoff finished, he dropped his pen down and stretched his arms over his head, groaning as the tension eased from his tight muscles. He loved being a solicitor but sometimes the job appeared to be all about the paperwork and less about the clients.

Standing, Geoff walked over to the window, placing a hand on the glass. The cold penetrated his skin, and he shivered at the difference in temperature. The study and his body were far warmer than outside. He sighed looking at the darkening sky. It seemed to be taking a long time for spring to arrive.

He turned, looking back at his desk, seeing the paperwork gathered on it. He was now part owner of his father's company, and he enjoyed the work but not the headaches that came with being the boss. He would rather be sat in court representing a client than dealing with the running of a business. He sighed walking back to his desk and sat down looking over the figures his accountant had sent him that morning.

When he heard a floorboard creak above him, he lifted his head and stared at the ceiling. Was Ben finally getting out of bed?

Geoff had only known Ben through Sebastian, an employee, due to his relationship with Tom. Seb and Tom had known each other as teenagers, but when Tom had been thrown out by his parents for being gay, they had lost touch.

Tom had spent four years on the street as a prostitute when Seb had seen him one night. Seb had pursued Tom, refusing to leave him to live that life, and during this time, they had fallen in love.

At the same time, a friend of Ben and Tom's, Adam, had been murdered. Ben, feeling guilty over his death, had attempted suicide. This, in turn, led Geoff to Ben when he'd helped Seb and Tom. And now Seb not only had Tom living with him but Matt and Luke, another two teenagers who had been living with Tom and Ben.

When Geoff had seen Tom's friend lying in that hospital bed, he knew he couldn't leave him there alone. Ben had been pale, thin, and the dark shadows under his eyes testified to the difficult life he'd been living. Geoff had made the decision to bring Ben back to his house when he was discharged from hospital so Geoff could aid him in his recovery after his failed suicide attempt.

The sound of the doorbell ringing dragged Geoff from his thoughts, and when he looked at the clock, he realised it was later than he'd thought. Getting up, Geoff took his glasses off and placed them on the desk before walking to the front door to answer it.

When he opened it, he found Seb and Tom stood there. "Hey, come in," he told them, holding the door open for them.

"We're not disturbing you, are we?" Seb asked as they walked in.

"No, not really. Just finishing my closing statement for the Peterson case and going over the figures," Geoff answered, closing the door behind them.

Seb was slightly taller than Tom, with black hair and hazel eyes. Tom had short blond hair, having recently cut it, and blue eyes. When Geoff had first met Tom, he'd been thin, but now he'd put weight on and looked much healthier for it. He'd lost the dark circles from under his eyes and had more colour in his cheeks, but Tom still appeared wary around Geoff.

"How's Ben been? Any better?" Tom asked as they walked through the house and into the kitchen.

Since Ben's release from the hospital, he'd isolated himself from everyone and remained in his bedroom. None of the others had been able to reach him, and it was causing some concern for Geoff. The last thing Geoff wanted was for Ben to attempt to end his life again. The isolation and apparent depression could cause Ben to do something he wouldn't under normal circumstances, or whatever normal had been for him while living on the streets.

"No change really. Ben still appears depressed, but, with him isolating himself to his bedroom, he hasn't had any real opportunity to attempt to harm himself again." After Adam's body had been found, Ben had felt responsible because he hadn't been there to watch his friend's back. It wasn't Ben's fault-- Adam had run off, and Ben hadn't been able to find him. Still, Ben appeared to feel like it was his fault that he had let his friend die and so had tried to kill himself.

"I know. It's been two months now, and I was hoping he would have started to come around. I wish I'd been there," Tom muttered.

"Hey, it wasn't your fault. We've talked about this, haven't we?" Seb said to him, hugging him close.

"Seb's right. From what you've told me, it appears, for whatever reason, Adam was taking unnecessary chances with his life. Why else would he have gone out and not waited for anyone to be there for him? He was aware of how dangerous the streets were," Geoff added. He knew how hard Seb had worked to help Tom move past his own guilt over Adam's death.

"I know, course I fuckin' know. But he was my friend, and I feel like I let him down, that if I'd been there things might have been different. The attack a couple of weeks before seemed to be some trigger that made him change. He was never that fuckin' reckless, well, not that I'd noticed."

"Come on, Tom. We can't change what's happened, can we? For now, we need to be there for Ben." Seb tried to comfort Tom, but it appeared that Tom still wasn't fully over what had happened either.

"Tom, have you thought about talking to someone about what you've been through?" Geoff asked him. He knew Seb had tried to arrange for Tom to see a counsellor, but so far he'd had no luck. Tom refused to talk to anyone. Geoff believed all four of them needed to talk about their experiences living on the streets. To discuss everything they had been through, what they had witnessed, and having to sell sex to survive. Geoff wasn't certain if it was something he could have done if he was in a similar situation and he admired the strength they all seemed to possess. None of them had turned to drugs. Well, with the exception of Adam.

It had only come out after his death that Adam had been using, and this may have contributed to his behaviour. It had been a shock to Tom, Matt and Luke to find out about Adam's drug use. Ben hadn't been told yet, and Geoff wasn't sure if he was ready to hear about it. Ben didn't need to know about that. He'd probably blame himself for that too.

"Not this again." Tom closed his eye briefly, rubbing his head. "I don't want to see or talk to anyone. Fresh start right? So why go over all of it? It's done. It's over." Tom swiped a hand out in front of him, staring at Seb and Geoff.

"How about a journal? I've read that sometimes if a person doesn't want to talk about what has happened in their life then writing it down can help. You could write down your experiences, what you went through. It might help with some things," Seb said to Tom.

"What? Is it gang up on Tom time? Well, I can tell you what you can do--"

"Don't get angry, Tom," Geoff interrupted. "We're just concerned for you. What you've been through will have left some mark, and Seb wants to help you. I was the one who suggested it, so don't be angry with him. If you want to be angry at anyone, be angry at me. You don't have to go and see anyone, but just think about it, alright?" Geoff paused, taking a deep breath in. "Now, what do you want to drink?"

Both asked for coffees and Geoff started the coffee machine. He could hear them talking quietly behind him and he didn't want to interrupt. It was clear that Tom was angry over what had been said, but Geoff believed that speaking to someone would help him.

Geoff liked Tom, and he made Seb happy, which he needed with everything that was happening with his parents. They still had issues with him being in a relationship with Tom. They still phoned the office to try and obtain information about Seb, how he was doing at work and what was happening in his life.

Seb's parents never mentioned Tom by name, simply referred to him as 'that boy' or 'it.' Why they couldn't speak to Seb directly confused Geoff. He was their son, and they had refused to talk to him because of his relationship with Tom.

Geoff knew Tom's parents had thrown him out for being gay, but he didn't know Ben's story yet. Ben barely spoke, barely ate or slept. He could hear him moving around his room at night and worse were the times when he could hear him cry. He'd lost count of the number of times he'd wanted to go into Ben's room and comfort him, but he knew Ben wouldn't want that. He wasn't ready for that yet. Ben didn't know him. Geoff was Seb's boss who had given him a place to stay after Adam's murder and Ben's subsequent failed suicide attempt. Geoff quietly sighed, finished making the coffee and handed Tom and Seb a mug each.

Take a Chance

"Do you want to go up and see him?" he asked Tom.

Tom nodded as he blew on his coffee. "Yeah, I will in a few minutes. I just need to warm up first. Can't believe how cold it is at the moment."

"Yes, it certainly is." Geoff paused, thinking of a way to ask Tom about Ben. He didn't want to upset him by asking personal questions, but he needed answers.

He cleared his throat. "Tom, do you know how Ben ended up on the streets? He hasn't talked much and if I'm going to be of any assistance to him, knowing some of his background would help."

Tom shook his head, pursing his lips. "No. We never really talked about stuff like that." Tom paused, frowning. "What we had wasn't that usual, I guess. I don't know many others who all lived together like we did, doing what we did." Tom shrugged. "But, I didn't hang out with many others. It was just a case of surviving really."

Geoff nodded, listening to Tom. Ben appeared to be a private individual, if he understood Tom correctly. Ben hadn't talked much, but the few words he'd spoken hadn't included anything about his family or friends. Geoff had asked some questions but realised quickly that Ben would clam up and then wouldn't talk at all. In fact, he barely looked him in the eye.

Being a solicitor helped. Geoff knew when to push and when to pull back. He knew how to ask the right questions in a non-threatening way. He would have to be patient and wait for Ben to trust him and then he would hopefully open up to him. All in good time.

"What was it like?"

Tom looked at him, and Geoff held his stare. He wanted to know what Ben had experienced. He watched as Tom clenched his jaw and his hand tightened on the mug he held.

"What do you think it was fuckin' like?" Tom snapped at him.

"You tell me, Tom. If I'm to be of any help to Ben, I need to know something of what you went through, how you lived."

Tom paused before speaking. "Sure, why not. It was a piece of piss. Easy--"

"Tom, don't be like this. Please," Seb spoke to him quietly.

"Look, I don't want an argument, but I do want to help Ben. Anything you can tell me will be kept between us." Geoff held his hand out palm upwards towards Tom.

"I don't want to talk about it. I don't want to have to go through all that shit again. It was fuckin' hard enough living it." Tom shook his head and sighed deeply. "Look, let me think about it, alright? I know you want to help him, just give me some time. It wasn't easy doing what we did. You had to learn to shut parts of yourself off when things happened to you, when you had to perform. That's why so many turn to drugs or get pissed. Living on the streets is fuckin' hard."

"Thanks. I appreciate it. I know I'm asking a lot of you, but I wouldn't have asked you if I didn't think it would help me in some way to understand where Ben is right now."

"Is he talking at all?" Tom asked him.

"Some, not much though. He's withdrawn and appears depressed. I have to force him to eat, otherwise he would starve. He rarely leaves his room and don't even ask me about his personal hygiene." Geoff shook his head.

"Sounds like depression," Seb commented after hearing Geoff's description of Ben.

Geoff nodded. "Yes. I'm fairly certain it is. That's why I want him to see a professional. He might need antidepressants, and I can't be here all the time to watch over him. I need to get back to the office and see everyone. If I thought it would help him, I'd have him come in and do some work. He seems intelligent, well, that's when we manage to have a conversation that lasts longer than five minutes."

"He is smart, very smart. I always wondered why he was on the streets, but he never talked about it. At all. None of us knows. Maybe he told Adam, but I guess we'll never know now." Tom put his mug down on the counter and turned to Seb. "I'm going up to see him."

Coming July 2017

About the Author

Megs Pritchard lives in England and is a mother to two small boys. When she isn't working or being mummy, she is busy writing about complex characters that know the harsh realities of life but want a HEA.

A lover of M/M and M/F romances she believes everyone deserves to be happy, healthy and loved.

Growing up in a military family, Megs has travelled Europe and has a great deal of respect and gratitude for all the men and women who have and who still serve. Her dream job was to be a Bomb Disposal Expert and even had her own 'kit' when she was younger.

She is currently working on her first full length series called Second Chances.

Take a Chance

Coming Soon

New Beginnings

Book Two in the Second Chances Series

Releasing July 2017

The Bonds Within

Book Three in the Second Chances Series

Releasing Oct 2017

Megs Pritchard

Contact Information

You can learn more about Megs' writing at:

http://www.megspritchardauthor.com

Or you can follow her on:

Facebook: https://www.facebook.com/megspritchardauthor/

Instagram: https://www.instagram.com/megspritchardauthor/

Twitter: https://twitter.com/megspritchard1

Tumble: https://www.tumblr.com/blog/megspritchard

Pinterest: https://uk.pinterest.com/megspritchard1/

Take a Chance

Printed in Poland
by Amazon Fulfillment
Poland Sp. z o.o., Wrocław